Inspired & Motivated

D'Juana L.
Manuel-Smith

Inspired & Motivated

An Emotional Journey Back To Me

This is a work of fiction. The events and characters described herein are imaginary and are not intended to refer to specific places or living persons. The opinions expressed in this manuscript are solely the opinions of the author and do not represent the opinions or thoughts of the publisher. The author has represented and warranted full ownership and/or legal right to publish all the materials in this book.

Inspired & Motivated
An Emotional Journey Back To Me
All Rights Reserved.
Copyright © 2015 D'Juana L. Manuel-Smith
v1.0

Cover Photo © 2015 thinkstockphotos.com. All rights reserved - used with permission.

This book may not be reproduced, transmitted, or stored in whole or in part by any means, including graphic, electronic, or mechanical without the express written consent of the publisher except in the case of brief quotations embodied in critical articles and reviews.

Outskirts Press, Inc.
http://www.outskirtspress.com

ISBN: 978-1-4787-6225-6

Outskirts Press and the "OP" logo are trademarks belonging to Outskirts Press, Inc.

PRINTED IN THE UNITED STATES OF AMERICA

Books by D'Juana L. Manuel-Smith

Relaxation for the Mind, Body & Soul
{Poems and Stories for the Passionate at Heart}

Inspired & Motivated
{An Emotional Journey Back To Me}

This book is dedicated to:

Inspiration & Motivation

Without the inspirations that show me the way, I would not be motivated to pursue my dreams. The drive to inspire and motivate others is what keeps me moving forward on the journey to enrichment. I found my muse in spite of obstacles and I plan to inspire and motivate you who read my words.

~ Inspiration comes from the life lessons we view in everyday life. Everyone has the ability to be an inspiration.

~ Motivation is the drive to be more than ordinary. Motivate your dreams to become reality.

~If your dreams are never realized, they will only exist as fantasy.

Author's Note

I've come to the realization that I write the way I do to create a world full of beauty, romance, excitement and imagination in most cases. Living in a time where hatred, crime, heartbreak, lies and fear run ramped.

I feel an urgency to escape!
Even if it's only for a short while.
Even if it's only in my head.

The poems featured in this book reflect the thoughts and emotions envisioned in the heart of a woman who desperately wants to change the repetitive patterns she finds herself living with. Through these words open a world she has never known. A world where her opinion makes a difference, her voice can be heard over the crowd and her feelings are worth sharing without hesitation or dread. The fact that these words and emotions brought life to a dreamer's inner most thoughts and are seen as stimulating by someone other than herself as building fire, passion, and a strength all so new has opened her eyes to a world of possibilities.

There is freedom in expression when it comes from the heart!

Included Poetry/Story Titles:

(Within the story)

*Dreams in Reality
*I Was So Sure
*There was once a reoccurring dream
*Waking Dream
*How Dare You
*Acceptance of Self
*I Didn't Realize
*Precious Child
*Lost Not Found
*Without a Doubt
*My Vow
*How Does It Feel?
*Mixed Emotions
*Look At Me Now
*Dirty Talkin'
*When the Muse Strikes
*He Makes Me Smile
*Finding My Way
*A lil piece of me
*He Planned the Perfect Evening

Included Poetry/Story Titles:

(Concludes the Book)

*Inspire & Motivate
*What Do I Do?
*On Your Wedding Day
*Pledge
*Best Friends
*Wife, Mother, and Teacher
*Always By My Side [To my B.F.Fs.]
*Willing To Share
*Let You In
*Just an Illusion
*Crime & Punishment
*Want What I Want
*Denial
*Worthy Praise
*Don't Count Me Out
*Inspirational Design
*Dimensions, Depth & Perception
*Barriers
*Patience
*I Want To Know
*Desire in Question
*Craving
*Will You Let Me
*State of Being

*Only I Can Hear It
* Not Afraid
*Gift
*My Life
*Trying Not To Complain
*Fragile
*Persuasion of the Mind
*Selfish (A Child's Starvation)
*Display of Love
*Out of My Head
*Writer's Block
*Why Do I Keep Coming Back
*Losing the Fight
*The End…?
*Power of a Voice
*Deserving
*Fear vs. Trust
*Dazed & Confused
*I Know Where I Come From
*Inspiring Notion
*This Stranger I Know
* Beyond the Wall
*When You Need Your Muse
*Frustration
*A Class with No Life
*Beyond the Hate
*Seasoned Learner
*Mirror Image

Prologue

I sit in my quiet space and write in a journal everything that brings me joy, pain, sorrow and even worry or anxiety. Mostly, passion and hope. Anything that makes my heart flutter let it be good or bad I write it in my journal.

I do have this secret wish though and that's to be a successful writer. Writing always gave me comfort and though I fear expressing my inner most thoughts and feelings to the world, I would love to know what it would be like to open up myself and share my views instead of hiding. I've always hid from others. Pleasing them was always what I did because criticism was such a large pill to swallow for me. I didn't know how to shout or be heard over the noise that surrounded me my whole life.

I always saw excitement. I dreamed passion. I never seized the day and I really wanted, no I needed to know what it would be to live life, My life to the fullest! As I write my emotions out, I can see the stories unfolding. I've created images in my head to accompany each line

I write. I wonder if what I recognize as a masterpiece could be seen the same in someone else's eyes.

How's this for a title...

"Inspire & Motive"
Poetry for the Heart & Mind
By, C.C.

Well here it is all put together just the way I want. The words flow nicely. Sketching and pictures allow you to see into my meanings. I wonder who, if anyone would understand where I come from? Would someone be able to understand my heart by reading my words?

Excitement seemed to be taking over me lately and I loved the charge it filled through me. Every word I wrote made me want to keep going. This should be published! I'm going to do it. I've already put most of it together and it looks pretty good. Now I just need someone to read it to.

Sadly I don't know anybody who'd be impartial. My time is so limited with taking care of the family that I don't have it or the money to spare to see it through just yet.

Oh, who am I kidding? This is a stupid idea. No one will ever want to hear what I have to say. These are just the sappy thoughts of a woman scared of speaking out loud. Maybe I should keep things to myself. I think I'll simply keep adding to my journal. Who knows what tomorrow will bring for me!

Dream deferred. But it will become reality!

Dreams in Reality

Dreams:
Life existing only in sleep
Reality:
Life existing unlike any dream

Living life in this reality is a wandering state of dreaming.
I live my life with outstretched fingers searching for the answers to my dreams.
Dreams that I fear are out of my reach because my reality is often too harsh.
The harsh reality of my life is that I am scared!
Scared that it will be too hard to make my dreams come true on my own.
I don't want to be alone!
In my dreams I am never on my own, but the reality of life is that your dreams are only reachable by your hands alone.
My reality has great influence on my dreams, good and bad. Although each reveals reversing roles, both play a part to my fantasies & nightmares. Often my fantasies end with tragic prophecy and the nightmares end with heroic triumph.
Real experiences colliding with imaginary dreams, forcing my mind to decipher their meanings.
These are the dreams that bring conflict in my reality.
I'm looking to my dreams for inspiring acts in realistic situation. However, what I dream seems an impossible feet once I awake. My experiences happen so readily and easily in a dream state. It's getting them to materialize in daily events

that I'm working on.
Wishing for my dreams to become my reality I find that I lose sight of what is real. Trying to rationalize fact from fiction, but determining the boundaries and wanderings of my mind allow me to set reachable, achievable dreams within my reality.

Journey Back To Me

When C.C. first saw Jesse she knew she had to meet him. There was something about him and for some reason she couldn't tell what team he was playing for. But some time passed and as the conversations picked up, the players slowly came up to bat. His game was tight and knew how to play the game.

As much as she resists she can never seem to turn her back on him. He's just so cute. Jesse always makes it a point to say hello and touch her ever so slightly, making C.C. sure of his intensions. "I can't deny it, I like how he makes me feel", she thought. They've gone out a few times, just drinks and a little flirting and it's been great. But this last time they couldn't help but get a little closer. Jesse smelled so good and C.C. has those beautiful eyes. They wanted and need to see how the other one kissed. "I couldn't believe it," they thought to themselves. It was more than either of them had expected. Neither of them knew what to say or do next. They decided to take a walk to clear their heads and go somewhere to make some since of what is really going on between them. The feeling between them seems to be building up inside, but what could be done about it? Could anything really be this real? Do they truly want more to come of the emotions they feel?

With all the questions coming to mind, only one question sticks out the most. How could we live with ourselves? You see, Jesse has a girlfriend and C.C. has a family of her own. Nothing was ever supposed to come out of them simply talking. They just wanted to get to know each other. Jesse always thought that until he was actually married he was never going to hurt anyone or get hurt himself. As for C.C. she's been feeling lonely and needed someone to talk to or to lean on. She always thought her marriage was solid and she couldn't love her husband and children more, but there is something missing from her life. She just couldn't explain it.

A while back C.C. had to deal with quite a few tragedies that wouldn't be solved with a, "mommy it's alright" or "honey, we can get through this." Hearing the same thing over and over from those who are expected to say soothing comments just wasn't enough. Jesse was getting the same kind of feelings but in reverse. Everyone was always pressuring him to be the strong one- the one to kiss it and make it all better. All he ever wanted was for someone to listen to him for a change, especially now that the realization of marriage was becoming more and more real to him. Don't misunderstand the dedication he has for his fiancé, he always knew they would be together, "but now something is changing in her that I'm not sure I'm ready to handle," he thought. Jesse's mind tended to wonder if he was absolutely ready to be tied down at such an early age. "I know I love her and would do anything for her, but is my love enough to really make it last," Jesse said. Lately the thought of the wedding made him want to run screaming. His world began crashing down around him all too fast. "I just need a breather," he screamed to himself.

When C.C. and Jesse met it was simply a change of pace for both of them and they saw nothing wrong with getting to be good friends. But now with everything going on in their separate lives the friendship they were building one day began to feel relaxed and more comforting in their time of need. However, the down side of it is that it's feeling too relaxed and comforting that it's no longer just confiding in one another.

"This is becoming dangerous," C.C. said nervously! "What I'm feeling for you was never supposed to feel so good," she told Jesse.

Jesse said, "What's wrong with feeling like this? Maybe what we thought was our lives, actually isn't the real thing", he questioned.

And because C.C. wasn't feeling so sure about her present life she tells Jesse that she needs to do some thinking. So she leaves him contemplating what he has said to her.

Later that week, C.C. tried to see whether or not

what he said was true. Was she living a lie and is this new relationship worth risking the hearts of her family to please her own? Just then, her phone rang and it was Jesse. C.C. really didn't know if she should talk to him, but her curiosity of him forced her to answer and when she did a huge smile came over her face. The sound of his voice made a big difference in her day and that was just what she needed especially now. You see, C.C's husband seemed to be getting more cross with her and she couldn't figure out why. He was always downing her and complaining about everything C.C. didn't do to make him happy. She always loved and supported this man and would do anything he needed her to do. But now that she needed some attention and understanding it's just too much of a bother on his part.

This is why talking to Jesse was making her feel good about herself. All she could do is say to him, "meet me at [?]" You see they had a secret place that they never spoke of in public and then she hung up the phone. When Jesse saw C.C. face to face he told her, "I needed you" and wrapped his arms tightly around her frame. He began to speak to her and she put her finger to his lips to stop him and kissed him so long and soft that neither wanted to let go. It was like they were never apart. Everything was perfect, almost like destiny.

"I am sorry for not calling", she said, "but I got scared of my feelings for you."

Jesse told her, "Don't be scared of how you feel for me because I feel exactly the same."

At this point no one or nothing mattered. They just had to be together even if it was for short periods of time: a phone call to say hi, a wave when passing by, or a walk whenever they had a spare moment. Every moment meant something other than the ordinary and that's what they both needed. They started spending more time than they actually had together and it felt really good. It was as if it was only the two of them in the world. C.C and Jesse tuned everyone and everything out. It all seemed to be making things better for them, more calming, more peaceful; however, their occasional visits weren't enough. Soon the two started meeting regularly. This made their lives change drastically, for the better at first. The kissing became longer and more passionate. Quiet dinners filled with interesting conversations about thoughts and dreams as if not a care in the world. Kisses encouraged caresses so tender they couldn't resist the desire to get closer intimately.

Jesse boldly asked C.C., "Do you want to go away with me?"

Without hesitation and sounding in a hurry she replied, "Where to?"

He told her, "Anywhere as long as I can hold you."

She answered him with an anxious, "Yes!", but in her mind she could hear her husband's voice.

Jesse looked at her wondering why she seemed

so unsure all of a sudden. He asked her if she really wanted to spend a romantic weekend with him and she said "Sure!" They made each other feel overjoyed and whenever they parted they ached to be together.

The Getaway

This was going to be perfect! But neither of them was thinking of the consequences that would await them. Physical comfort was all they wanted right now. Jesse and C.C. thought up reasons for leaving town for a few days although lame it worked. It was like high school or a honeymoon without the commitment. They decided to catch a train to Vermont to a small bed & breakfast. The train ride was quiet and it gave them a chance to learn a little more about just everyday goings on. Jesse held C.C. in his arms the whole trip. It started out beautifully. Just then, for some reason Jesse's phone rang, it was his fiancé checking in on him, asking about the business trip and for suggestions about the wedding invitations. That put a damper on their plans. He got up so that he wouldn't make C.C. feel bad. She didn't mind, but she only wondered why her husband hadn't called to check on her. This only made her get angry and realize why she decided to take the trip in the first place.

When they arrived at their room neither knew what to do first. It was just a matter of going for it. The temptation was so strong and there was no stopping them. They had all weekend. Jesse brushed C.C's hair back and gently caressed her face. He pulled her close into him and began to kiss her, first on the lips then on her neck. Suddenly he reached for the buttons on her blouse. He stopped for a minute looking into her honey brown eyes as if to ask for permission to continue. She made no move to stop him so he continued by sliding her blouse off of her shoulders rubbing and nibbling as he moved around her. C.C. wanted Jesse to rip all of her clothes off. She couldn't wait any longer! She turned around to undo his shirt and glided her fingertips across his broad chest. C.C. was very curious to see how soft the rest of his body actually was. He then took down her skirt massaging her thighs inside and out. Jesse kneeled in front of her and grabbed her derrière so strongly she held her breath and was scared to move. He kissed her navel and she let her body go into his arms. She then fell down to her knees to come face to face with him. They stared into each other's eyes. Then C.C. leaned into Jesse and landed a kiss on him that they both fell to the floor. C.C. lay there on top of Jesse rubbing her body up and down as they kept kissing so intensely. They wanted this closeness and did not care about what was happening around them. Jesse turned C.C. over onto her back and just stared at her. Her body quivered as he took the rest of her clothes off and she helped him with his. Comfort was just what they wanted from each other.

Contemplation

All of their troubles and worries disappeared when they were together. He treated her with kindness and respect and she listened without overbearing him. This is all they ever wanted. This went on for some time and neither one minded it at all. True their consciences were questioning them, but the happiness they felt when together made the two ignore their gut.

Whenever Jesse and C.C. returned home it was like a cloud came over them. C.C. stayed close to her children just to avoid the constant abuse she felt from her husband. No matter how hard she tried nothing was good enough.

"Why should I bother?" she thought. But naturally he took it as neglecting him. So he would scream and bluster about how no one does what he expects of them or not showing him his proper respect.

One day, C.C. couldn't take it anymore and she got up to reach for the phone to find her peace of mind. Just then she paused, for what might happen if she dialed the numbers? But little did she know Jesse was feeling the pressure back home as well. He became so bogged down with pending wedding plans he was on the verge of calling it all off. All he wanted to do was spend some alone time with his fiancé to be sure their love was still as strong. However, every time he would try to talk to her about anything else she didn't have the time. This was getting very frustrating.

"I can only do but so much," he thought to himself. Jesse got up to go be alone and all of a sudden his phone rang. He didn't recognize the number at first, but he answered it anyway. When he picked up Jesse hoped whoever it was did not want to talk about the price of the wedding cake or tuxedo fittings.

He said hello, but no one spoke. Just when he started to hang up the person cleared their throat on the other end. He said, "I'm happy it's you!" Somehow he knew it was C.C. Jesse said, "Why didn't you say anything?"

"I didn't know what to say," said C.C. Both of them were glad to hear from one another. Neither knew exactly what to say, but it didn't matter, it was a sigh of relief to know that they still had such a bond between them.

It would be some three months before they would see each other again. They thought that only speaking on the phone was best, giving their situations, at least for a while. Wedding plans and being a homemaker were more in the forefront than trying to steal a few precious moments with one another. So instead of thinking of themselves they put all of their concentrations on home. This was the right thing to do to keep everyone happy. But was it the right thing for them? They had to be sure! This time apart made them ponder how they first met and the circumstances to which this relationship has blossomed.

How It All Began

Jesse wanted so much to reconnect with his fiancé, to find why he fell in love in the first place. He continued to go through with the nuptial plans, but was exhausted by being ignored whenever he asked to spend quality time together. She would tell him he wasn't concerned with the wedding or helping to make things special for this important day. Jesse desperately wanted to feel needed for more than his choice in color swatches.

"I need you here with me," he shouted. "Talk to me!" She looked at him with confusion, rolled her eyes and walked away. How could he make her understand what he even means?

On C.C.'s home front things could be going better. She spent every waking day waiting on her husband and the children hand and foot. Breakfast, lunch, dinner, washing, cleaning, and shopping. She went back and forth to special activities or events for everyone except her. Every time C.C. would sit down someone was screaming for her. Her only private time was in the bathroom and this wasn't exactly private because her husband would just walk in, "Just had to get something," he would say. It was as if she didn't matter in their world, she simply existed to acknowledge them at no thought to herself.

"I can't even pee in private!" she yelled.

Her husband came barging in again screaming even louder, "What the hell are you yelling for?" "Hurry up I have to get in there," without closing the door.

Tears streaming down her face she finished and went on with her chores.

I Was So Sure

I used to know what I wanted
My life was mapped out with clear directions
I followed all the rules without error
But something changed my path selection
I was so sure my way was the right one

I loved with all of my heart
I gave of myself without hesitation
I was so sure my decisions were correct
What was it I was missing?

My journey was heading towards the future
My future consisted of a lasting love
With a family growing happy and strong
But somewhere it detoured
And I'm not sure how to get back on track

I was so sure I found what I was looking for
I never felt lost ~ I knew where to go
But there was a crash ~ I was blind-sided
I made it out with a few bruises ~ I'd live
But when I got to where I was going ~ I wasn't wanted

I was so sure: (repeat with each line)
What I wanted was clear
I could be loved in return
That my future wouldn't be lonely
Someone would want to find me

How could this neglect and disrespect be constantly tolerated? Surely this was not the life they chose, full of loneliness and hatred and misery? Where was the love and consideration? But this was the life that C.C. lived every day. Constant interruptions as if she wasn't doing something important and it was driving her insane! Questioning everything she said or did with the assumption that something must be going on behind his back.

For weeks now C.C.'s husband accused her of being lazy, forgetful, or plain ole useless. She finally started to find comfort in writing as a way to release her anger and sadness and above all loneliness. It wasn't much but she breathed easy when she set pen to paper. She freely spoke her mind with no criticism. Because she got lost in her thoughts, her own thoughts, she relaxed a little more and took more and more time for herself. Her husband of course took this to mean, oh who knows what he thought it meant, all he knew was that he was no longer the center of her attention and the kids were asking him to help or do more with them.

"C.C. where are you?" he would scream.

One day when the kids were at school C.C. decided she would go out for a walk and sit in the local coffee house to do a little writing. However, this particular day her husband decided to come home earlier so he could get some extra time to rest by himself. But to his dismay, the school called home to say that someone needed to pick up one of the kids who had gotten sick. This made him very angry!

"You hear me calling you!"

C.C. did not plan on being very long, only an hour or so but it was an hour longer than he thought she needed to be. Whenever she left the house C.C. made sure her cell phone was with her in case of emergencies. Her husband bought her one so he could reach her when he needed her to do something. He made sure it was in his name so he could monitor it of course. When C.C.'s husband realized she wasn't home he stormed out to go to the school and angrily called to see where she was and why she wasn't at home.

After riding a few blocks from the house and before he could finish dialing the number he came to a stop sign and noticed someone familiar in the shop on the corner. It was C.C. He saw her talking to a man then taking his card, scribble something on a napkin and gave it back to the man. Her husband was furious! He zoomed through the intersection to get the kids from school.

As for Jesse, why did he feel so alone in this relationship? Jesse was finding it hard to stay in love with his fiancé or even worse, remember why he fell in love in the first place? Every conversation was one sided with her.

One night he said to her, "Let's go out tonight, just you and me."

She hesitated at first but agreed just the same. Jesse thought he would try to rekindle what he felt they were losing. He thought he might take her to a restaurant for dinner, drinks, and dancing.

"This place is lovely. How did you find it?" she said eagerly.

Jesse just looked at her dumbfounded. "This is where we met." The fact that he had to tell her this shocked him! "Don't you remember any of that?" He thought to himself, "Surely she couldn't forget how we met? Is our love truly fading away? She is so worried about this wedding, she is forgetting about me and us!"

Purposely By Mistake

Today would be the turning point in Jesse and C.C.'s lives. C.C. had found her opportunity to possibly have her work published, whereas Jesse found someone who had a passionate heart as he did. Jesse was an up and coming book editor in a small publishing house and was interested in C.C.'s pending writings. They met in a coffee shop and exchanged numbers. She was so excited that her words were thought to be inspiring. He couldn't resist reading some of her entries of her would be book, for her words spoke of love and desire. Jesse hadn't heard such passion from a prospective writer since he started working at this company. Truthfully he hadn't heard this much passion from anyone in a long time. As a publisher this could not be passed up. After sharing contact information they set up an appointment to meet.

C.C. was so excited to have someone interested in reading her work. Jesse seemed to really favor and understand what she wrote about.

"You write beautifully", he said.

"Why, thank you", she replied. "I love writing. I

pour all my emotions into my work."

"Do you always speak of passion and love?" he asks.

"Only when I'm not hurting inside," she says.

"Oh, that's very interesting," Jesse says raising an eyebrow. "Do you hurt more than you love?" he asks.

"I'd rather not say," she whispers. "But writing is an escape from my hurting," C.C. says sadly.

"Please forgive me, I don't mean to pry. I just wondered, what were your inspirations when coming up with such lyrical impressions?" Jesse asked almost concerned.

"Well to tell you the truth, I write about my feelings or experiences either encountered or fantasized," she said. She blushes and Jesse notices.

The two of them had a few more meetings together discussing the creation of C.C.'s book. The more personal touches added to the book the more personal information was revealed about C.C. and Jesse became very interested in who she was. He wanted to know more of this beautiful person whose emotional side he was being drawn to.

Jesse hung on every word she said. He wasn't use to hearing someone speak so eloquently and assured on matters of the heart. His fiancé wasn't big on sharing how she felt. Jesse really missed being told what it's like to love, be in love, and desired above all, in all things. With each intimate phrase C.C. read aloud Jesse would sigh and then C.C. would blush and squirm in her chair. They both started to realize the affects generating from such tantalizing expressions.

This was all new to C.C. She had no idea her thoughts would get this kind of response. C.C's husband hardly paid attention to her any more, let alone took time to listen to her thoughts. This made C.C. look forward to these precious moments with Jesse. The attraction between the two of them was obvious and the chemistry that heated when they were together was intense to say the least!

Some time passed between their meetings and it was going great. The production process was coming along smoothly and their personal connection was growing as well. The amount of time they shared was extending with each visit. They were working, but it was fun and different and a breath of fresh air. Their focus was on this new book and not on the things they wish could be left behind. Jesse and C.C. enjoyed each other's company so much that they decided they would spend some time outside of the office setting and have lunch to relax from the hard work going into the book. This lunch would certainly not be the last time they spent outside of work. They had a bond that was pulling them closer on a new level now.

Jesse found he was staring at her longer and C.C. fawned over the fact that he was so gentle and understanding of her feelings. Both wanted to reach out to try and hold hands or even kiss. Their urges to resist one another were becoming harder with each visit. But for now they played it innocent.

Although it was a while since they last saw each other they could not go without speaking to one another. The frustration and loneliness was so deeply embedded within them that it seemed there was no other way to be happy or smile. The next time that they spoke they suggested that they meet to discuss the finalization of the book and to see where things were heading with them. They just had to be face to face. They had to be sure if giving up on their existing lives was worth ending. But staying in unhappy relationships couldn't be better. True, there is a lot to consider and it would be selfish not to weigh their options carefully.

The Confession

"I've tried to make things work at home, but I always have this anxious feeling in the house," she admitted during one of their meetings. "When I'm with you I can be myself. I can say what's on my mind and you don't judge me," she confessed to Jesse. "I try to share my thoughts with my husband, but he seems to be more distant than usual."

C.C. couldn't help the feeling that her husband was cheating on her again, yet making it seem as if she was the problem. Jesse always listened intently though when C.C. needed to talk. He liked having someone trust him and need him for comfort.

"I feel the same way," he replied sadly. For someone about to be married, the distance between he and his fiancée was becoming great. He desperately wanted the closeness he felt with C.C.

Do I Know You?

One day, C.C. got a call from an unknown number as she worked on a few new entries sitting in the café. She picked up cautiously not recognizing the number. It was her daughter's teacher. This was strange because she calling from a cell phone number instead of one of the school's numbers. She introduced herself as Annette Hall.

"Would it be possible for us to meet," she said.

"I need to speak with my husband and check my schedule first", C.C. said in response.

"Ok, you can call me at this number any time is good. It's so hard to get messages from the main office."

Later that day C.C. called back to give her a time and day to meet, but when she called a man answered.

The man said, "Hello."

C.C. said, "Hi."

There was a pause. He said hello again, this time softly. C.C. asked to speak to Ms. Hall.

He raised his voice and called, "Annie, phone for you."

She took a long sigh. There was a strange feeling creeping upon her. They spoke for a few minutes discussing the best time to meet agreeing to see one another soon.

I Should Have Known

Things were tense at home for C.C. Her husband took some getting used to the idea of C.C. writing a book and always being out of the house and unavailable. She had been late a few times picking up the kids so her husband had to stop his plans to get them and tend to their needs himself. This was making him angry.

"Your mother should be here with you!"

He usually says this, not because the children need him, but as he doesn't want to be bothered.

"Now I have to pick them up." He tends to murmur loudly when he's upset.

This knowledge made C.C. more eager to write out her frustrations and be out of the house. She wasn't surprised, this has happened before, but there was something different about his mood swings lately.

Jesse had some news to deal with as well. True, he wasn't told to his face, but it was news just the same and had no clue how to approach it. Going over some publications for review in his home office he overheard a conversation. He tried to stay busy so as to avoid more wedding talk. The discussion became a little more heated and quietly went to the door to listen.

"How could you let this happen? Do you know

what he will do if he finds out?"

He couldn't make out the voices at first. Just then he heard someone say,

"Annie, do you know how far along you are?"

He almost slammed into the door!

Jesse screamed, "WHAT" and swung the door open. With wide eyes his fiancée turned to look at him to find Jesse with a blank expression. Neither knew what to say and continued to stare.

Once the fact that she was pregnant was finally admitted to him, he simply accepted this new level of stress. But as time passed something just wasn't sitting right with him. She wouldn't give him any information on how she and their child were progressing. She seemed to be rushing around more than ever, but only where this wedding was concerned.

He wondered, "Why won't she talk about the baby?" She would retort with answers like, "I just want to get the wedding out of the way, then we can concentrate on this baby." Jesse was feeling even farther apart from her now and didn't know why.

The Meeting

On a short notice meeting to decide on the cover of her book, Jesse felt the need to explain his standoffish behavior with C.C. He told her that he just found out that his fiancée was expecting. There was silence between them for a minute.

She exclaimed, "I can see how that can take your mind off of work." She really didn't know what to say. "I'm a little distracted myself. My husband is cheating on me."

The silence was back and stretched on a while longer. Out of nowhere C.C. asked why this meeting had been changed.

"I had to find a babysitter, because my husband said he was going to be late for a doctor's appointment and couldn't keep the kids."

Jesse turned to look at her and replied almost guiltily, "I have one too, to check things out for the baby." That eerie feeling crept across the room again. They quickly finished their task and said their goodbyes. It was the briefest encounter they ever shared.

C.C. made it back home before her husband did

and was glad because she didn't want to fight today. She got a call from him just as she settled to start dinner.

"Are you home? I'll be there soon. I need you.... DAMN IT! Can you watch where you're going?" He shouts as he crashes into someone leaving the doctor's office not paying attention.

"What's the problem?" C.C. asks.

"Somebody else holding me up that's all." He continues, "I need you to..." with his usual demands of her then hangs up the phone.

A few days later, Jesse calls C.C. because he wanted to let her know that her cover was ready to be proofed and to apologize for how their last meeting went. They chatted in that way that made them feel so comfortable, but neither mentioning the issues they were dealing with. As the conversation went on, she innocently asked him how his doctor's appointment went. This made them stop everything.

He looked directly at her and she said, "I'm happy for you."

Wearily he answered, "It was ok." He proceeded to explain the ordeal.

"I was hurrying for my appointment and was just barely knocked down by this rude guy pushing his way through the door just as I entered."

C.C. giggled a little. The tale seemed to spark a memory. He explained that he had to get blood work done along with his wife and the baby through an amniocentesis to check for any possible defects or something. Jesse seemed to be confused about the whole thing. So she moved on to happier topics and concluded their meeting once again.

The Realization

C.C. had a long day ahead of her. Dropping kids at school, grocery shopping, and a long list of errands that included going to the dry cleaners. Bringing the suits in to be cleaned she noticed some papers in the pockets. So she removed them before handing them over. Checking to see if they were important, C.C. unfolded one and it read: "**Appointment with Annie**." This was the same day as his doctor's appointment. He didn't mention meeting anyone else. She couldn't disguise her rage.

"He told me he had a doctor's appointment!" C.C. yelled and stormed out of the store.

The confusion was fogging her mind. Tired of putting up with the lies and harsh treatment and neglect from her husband she raced home with full intention of confronting him when he returned home. This was going to be the last straw! She had proof this time that he was cheating on her and wanted answers now. When arriving home, ready to yell and scream she began to calm slightly. It would be time to get the kids from school soon and mustn't let them see her so upset, so she decided to put it off until they were alone.

The feelings C.C. were holding in with great hardship led her to compose some new material. Her frustrations always eased when she set down to write. She put the kids to bed because it was getting late. By the time he finally would come home she couldn't even begin to question him. The need to know was no longer important. C.C. continued writing. The words read:

"It's said that when a woman cries over her man, she cares of the reasons why. But if she just smiles and walks away, she has no need to stay."

Just then her husband walked in the door. He asked her what she was doing. She simply looked up and replied dryly, "Working. Your dinner's in the oven." There was silence as he stared at her. "I'm going to bed." Nothing needed to be said.

"What was that?! C.C. woke with a start in a cold sweat. Her heart was racing and couldn't understand why. Then she began to calm her breathing and it all became clear. It was the reoccurring dream again. She jumped out of bed and ran to find her notebook to quickly write it down. She set the pen to paper and recited:

There was once a reoccurring dream...

I answer my phone in shock because I can see your face. You have your seductive, come-hither eyes glowing at me and say, "Hello, how are you?" We exchange seemingly pleasant, innocent conversation but being that I can see you on the phone, I notice your expression and tone of voice has altered into a very familiar sensual tone. I almost stop breathing when you ask to see me. "Meet me somewhere", you reply. Butterflies beat in my stomach the way they did when I was young and newly in love with you. I can't help but ask myself, why you would want to see me? Ulterior motive or to tease me further knowing what you do to me? Never able to resist your smile, of course I agree. I drive to meet you but I'm not alone. I don't know why, maybe I'm nervous. When I reach the destination it's a loud public place and I have to search for you. My phone rings again and once more it's your sultry voice telling me where to find you. Anxiously, I search through a crowded room and suddenly am stopped in my tracks. "There you are. I've been waiting for you," you call just from behind me. When I turn around you're leaning against a wall watching me intently. I can't help my blushing smile! You take my hand and we walk back to the car. Reaching there, noticing someone else is there as well, you mention, "I thought we'd be alone." Impishly I blink and shrug my shoulders. Apparently this doesn't faze you because you turn on me, starring deeply into my eyes, then lean closer to me pressing your lips against mine harshly and so suddenly that I gasp, opening my mouth allowing you instant entry intensifying your kiss. My emotions are scattered! Elated rapture is at the forefront of my stimulation. Although my questioning mind wonders why we are here? It makes me pull away. We sit in silence glaring at one another.

Time fast forwards as if I blackout. The silky brush of a rose petal is what sparks my eyes open. As I open my eyes to focus on the scene, we are alone. I'm sitting across from you at a table laden with glasses of wine, fresh fruit and fragrant candles. I am speechless and your smile lights up my heart.

You kiss me chastely on my mouth and I melt. Sitting here I notice a laptop on the table. What could it be for? Once I ask what it's for, you say, "It's a surprise," piquing my interest further. I still don't know why I'm here. This is so confusing! As I love every second of being in your presence and your touch, the thought that you don't want me anymore dashes my interlude like a scorching needle. The question is out of my mouth before I realized my spoken thought. "Why am I here? I thought you were over me." Suddenly I am in your arms. I hate that I could never resist you!

You hold me close, kiss a certain tickling spot, and sit me back in the chair. After pressing a button on the laptop a slideshow begins. All I hear is beautiful music, songs reminding me of so much joy. Then images flash on the screen. One by one, images of us that I'd almost forgotten and some construed to depict special events or occurrences I've never seen before. A story is playing out for me, but I don't know why. What does this all mean? The last image is of you actually kneeling before me holding a ring. I don't understand! This isn't a real image, it has never happened. I used to delude myself with this fantasy. But it falls back because of my knowledge of you not wanting to be with me. He's never asked me to marry him, so why now? Why this sudden change of heart? The stunned expression on my face prompts an explanation. He gazes into my eyes, pauses and tells me, "I love you." Of all our times together I never truly remember him saying the words. He continues, "I never stopped. And when you left me I realized it even more. I wanted to marry you for some time, but you were no longer mine." Tears begin to prick my eyes. All I ever wanted to be was his. I left him because I was so hurt. But my love for him wouldn't allow me to fully let him go. I respond, "I could have been. I wasn't good enough before and you broke my hurt." The tears roll continually now. "Please don't cry," he whines trying to calm me. "I want to prove myself. Prove that I can be worthy to have you as my own. I want to marry you," he says more persistently. I run my fingers down his smooth cheek. He closes his eyes and leans into my hand and I do the same. "I should never have let you go. Be mine!" There's been so much time apart and I don't know if I'm really available for this. How could I actually be considering this man? He hurt me deeply! But the love I had and maybe still hold for him is so overwhelming. The intense emotions for this creature have always enveloped my heart. It is what has kept me from hating him so. "Say something," he cries, bringing me out of my reverie. But I can't think of how to respond. My mind starts to cloud over. In my heart I'm screaming FINALLY! My mind is keeping me rooted in place and mute. There's too much baggage loaded with fear.

The fog is slowly consuming me. What's wrong? I want to... "Talk to me," he says smoothly. Why can't I speak?! I'm still... Cautiously he asks, "Do you love me?" I close my eyes again releasing newly unshed tears and am plunged into darkness. Wait! I can hear him shouting, "Stay with me, I need you!" What's happening? I feel so near, but no sound comes. My breathing is rapid, shallow with anxiety and anticipation. This is where I want to be and all my dreams realized in an instant. Tears are streaming down my face. It's the only physical affect I'm conscious of. Suddenly the darkness becomes silence and I feel lonely and empty. Whereas only moments ago, full elation swept through me like never before.

Defiantly my eyes spring open to the sun gleaming through the windows. Was this a dream? What just happened? I am still crying. This couldn't be simply a dream! It was so lucid and fact based. Maybe it's a revelation in disguise. I thought I was content in my heart, but perhaps I'm looking for a little more. A little more adoration, more desire and longing. This man I know very well. Explicit memories are attached to my emotions in his case. Where did this all come from? I fall back onto the bed and close my eyes again to be in front of this man to answer him at last. Just then my phone rings. Annoyed, picking up the phone I gasp to catch my breath. I can see him! It's him actually on my phone. When I answer it, I can hear that same sultry, seductive tone of voice saying, "Hello. How are you?" Using no filter I respond, "This can't be real! Is it really you?" He retaliates in saying, "Of course. Meet me somewhere."

As she was writing the dream down she thought to herself, 'Why did I just finish the most intense dream I ever had about you? You have never been so interactive with me. Very vivid! It just kept continuing. I jumped up and realized it wasn't real so went back to sleep and began where I left off. I'm confused as to the way I know or think you feel about me. Something I use to wish you would feel say or do to and with me happened in my dream. Why now? Why now am I having these dreams of my husband?

An Awkward Moment

A week after the doctor's appointment Jesse asked his fiancée if there was any news on the results from the blood work they'd received. He thought there would be a call or something by now to tell them if everything was ok. As usual she brushed it off as if it wasn't important.

"The nurse said I should be getting results by phone call. You haven't heard anything?" He looked at her questioningly. "What's the matter?"

"Nothing," she murmured. "They said they were calling to give you the results?" she stumbled when asking him.

"Yes, they asked for my number."

Jesse was beginning to become worried. Truthfully her reaction and answers were becoming maddening. He raised his voice when asking,

"What's wrong with you? Why wouldn't they call me? I would hope someone will be contacting me about me and my baby Annie!"

She said, "Of course, I thought they were just going to let me know. That's all." Apprehension stole over him, but he let it rest. However, this was far from over.

Next day at work Jesse had a break in meetings so decided to do some research of his own on amniocentesis. When reading he found that one isn't performed so early unless known health issues are possible or a paternity test is requested. He couldn't read any more. Concentration was gone at this information. There was a knock at the door.

"Come in," he shouted.

"Hello, am I disturbing you?"

He looks up to see C.C. standing over his desk. Jesse smiled sadly.

"Is everything alright? I could come back."

"No please, have a seat. I wasn't expecting you. This is a nice surprise."

"I just needed to drop some things off at the printers and just wanted to see you as well." She had been feeling so lost and alone lately. A friendly face was what would help.

"I'm glad you're here. I've been meaning to call you," he says walking around to stand in front of her.

"I wish you had," C.C. whispered with tears in her eyes.

She needed comforting and she wanted it from Jesse. C.C. jumped up and wrapped her arms around Jesse's neck tightly. He could feel her shaking.

"What's the matter, C.C.? Talk to me."

After a moment she tried to contain her sobs and

replied, "I don't know how much more of this I can take."

She went on to tell him her suspicions and recent findings. They sat for a short while. He let her vent.

"What sort of evidence do you have that he's cheating? Maybe he just forgot to tell you about the meeting."

"My daughter told me he said it out loud, and then I found her name in his pockets."

Neither said anything.

Quietly Jesse asks C.C., "Have you ever had an amniocentesis?"

"That seems like a strange question," she responded.

"I'm sorry, forget about it."

Simultaneously they sighed. They looked into each other's eyes not needing to say any more.

"I have to go," she said. Standing to escort her out he asked if it would be alright if he called her. She simply nodded and turned to leave fearful she would cry again.

Later this evening, there was a parent teacher conference and both C.C. and her husband needed to attend. This meant they were forced to be together and possibly have to speak. Because of her suspicions and anger, she really had nothing to say to her husband and he rarely had anything to say to her. However, there seemed to be something weighing on his mind more than usual.

Although they didn't want to endure this obvious show they needed to put on, it was unavoidable. A short time ago one of her daughter's started acting out in school. She was always so quiet and respectful. But they got a note asking to come in and discuss her recent behavior. She had been screaming at other kids being very aggressive when she wanted her way. She even slapped someone for annoying her, which was the main reason for the meeting.

C.C. and her husband reached the school. They found the class for Miss Hall and had to wait a few minutes for their appointment. The two tried to at least be civil and make small talk.

"This never used to be a problem for us," C.C. thought sadly.

She didn't realize she said it out loud. Instantly their heads snapped towards one another. He looked as if he was going to say something smart, but he actually stopped to look into C.C.'s eyes and they were teary.

He sighed and replied, "I know." Seeming to understand and read her mind.

All at once his demeanor softened and he grasped her knee quickly then released it just as quick. Unsure of C.C.'s reaction to this contact, he straightened up and stared off. She stares at him for a moment longer and a tear strayed down her cheek.

Just then, the classroom door opened and Miss Hall stepped out. She quickly glanced at C.C. and her husband and did a double take. C.C. thought this to be a little odd. The next few seconds seemed to play out in slow motion. She turned to her husband and he fractionally widened his eyes.

"Are you alright?" C.C. asked.

When she turned back Miss Hall seemed to go cold. She straightened up and reached her hand out to shake C.C.'s. As they shook hands C.C. felt Miss Hall tremble.

Miss Hall said shakily, "How do you do?"

Before C.C. could respond she said, "You're so cold, are you ok?"

"Yes, yes. Please come in and have a seat," gaining her composure quickly, but nervously.

They sit down in front of the teacher's desk. He keeps darting his eyes from C.C. to Miss Hall and she keeps blinking fast. Suddenly C.C.'s husband speaks up.

"I didn't know you were my daughter's teacher." Almost through gritted teeth.

Now it's C.C.'s turn to look between the two of them.

"Do you know each other?"

He said, "Umm..."

Miss Hall cut across him and answered, "We met here at school."

"But I thought you didn't know she was our child's teacher."

"I didn't. I helped her with a flat tire."

"Yes, and he was a big help," she replied with a

wide smile.

There was silence for a moment. A long deep sigh amongst the room. Then Miss Hall began to discuss the issues at hand with a little more ease and professionalism. They sit and listen to how their daughter has been behaving.

"Her general attitude has changed. She seems to be angry," Miss Hall adds with a confused expression. She begins, "Has there been any problems at home?"

Just as she asks, C.C. notices that she glances at her husband and rapidly stares back at C.C. saying,

"Oh please forgive me, I don't mean to pry."

"No!" he pipes up and C.C. exclaims,

"Well, everyone has problems, but I can't put my finger on anything," lowering her voice a little ashamed.

Miss Hall continues, "Has your daughter ever mentioned any concerns she may be having or show signs of acting out at home?" She peers cautiously at C.C.'s husband.

"I haven't noticed anything really," he responds.

C.C. cried, "She's more quiet than usual actually."

The three of them come to an understanding and agree to work together to get through to their daughter. They conclude their meeting. As they rise, the husband reached for the teacher's hand this time. C.C. began feeling a little overwhelmed, so she simply said 'thank you' and started walking away.

As she reached the door she heard Miss Hall say, "Nice to see you again and thank you for coming."

C.C. turned toward them and they let go of each other's hand. Miss Hall's phone rang as they were walking out of the class.

"Hi, Jess. I'm ready to go when you are."

C.C. paused feeling a tingle, then continued walking, shaking it off. She and her husband left together in silence.

Eye Contact

On the drive home C.C. kept glancing at her husband. He wouldn't turn to look at her directly. This made her apprehensions grow more evident.

"So you do know her or meet her before?"

"Why would you say that?"

She narrowed her eyes at him.

"I heard her say, 'Nice to see you again' and you claimed you helped her."

He jerked his neck to face her then back towards the road.

"Well, I've seen her when I dropped the kids off before and I forgot about the flat."

Through gritted teeth she questioned, "Why didn't you mention that to me? Either of you?

Sensing C.C's eyes on him, he merely shrugged his shoulders and headed home. She fisted her hands in her lap. What's the big secret? He was just going to deny knowing her. The thought kept playing in her mind.

Doubt

"What's wrong with you? You've been a little anxious since we got home."

Jesse was becoming more and more worried, if not suspicious of his fiancé. She was jumpy and moody even for a pregnant woman. Every time the phone rang she would run to answer it first. It was really starting to annoy him, so he asked,

"Have you heard from the doctor yet?"

She murmured, "No, I wish they would hurry."

Jesse said, "Do you think something is wrong with the baby?"

She began nervously, "Oh I don't know, the waiting is just making me crazy!"

"Would you like me to call and ask...?"

But before he could even finish his question she cut across and said, "No, No I'm sure everything is fine. I just need to have a little patience. I'll calm down."

She patted Jesse soothingly on his chest. They stared at one another for a moment then gave a swift hug before going off to finish their own tasks.

Reveal

About a week later, C.C. was running some errands. When she came into the house her daughters were running upstairs. The oldest was crying again. C.C. called to them, but they didn't answer. She put the bags down in the kitchen and she spies her husband finishing a phone call looking extremely agitated. Continuing to unpack her load, she sighs long and deep.

After turning to face her husband there is a pause then she asks, "So what happened? Why is she crying? They seemed so upset."

He actually sucked his teeth and stomped passed her in the kitchen to the refrigerator, grabbed a beer then slammed it. After he took a swig he grunted,

"I don't know. I was on the phone and my conversation got a little heated and I yelled at them."

They went back and forth with each other.

"Why would you do that? You know how upset she's been. Did they do something to you?"

"I don't need this right now! I didn't mean to yell at them", he says a little more evenly and pauses in his tirade.

"Just forget it. I'll go and speak to them myself," she says as she walks away from him.

Storming upstairs she is on a mission, but for some reason the fuming anger building inside makes her thoughts cloudy. C.C. tries to calm and focus on the needs of her daughters. Before going into their rooms she takes a deep breath, and then cautiously opens the door.

Comes To the Light

When she walks in the oldest girl is still whimpering lying on the bed. C.C. sits beside her to comfort her.

"Please talk to me."

"Mommy, she said she doesn't want to be here." The younger responds upset for her sister.

"What! Why?" Trying to turn the girl toward her, she sits up to face C.C. with tears still in her eyes. "Talk to me baby. What's got you so upset lately?"

Hesitantly she says, with a stammer, "Daddy doesn't love us."

C.C. gasps with wide eyes.

"Why do you think that? That's just not true," she whispers unsure of her own answer. "Has he ever said that to you?"

"Not to me."

"Well then how...?"

She cut across her mom, "But I heard him on the phone!"

"What!"

"The first time..."

C.C.'s eyes widen with alarm, "I heard him talking about getting away from us to be with her."

C.C.'s heart nearly stopped.

"Are you sure about that?"

"Yes, mommy I'm sure. He called her Annie when he talked about their doctor's appointment."

The room began to spin and fire burned through C.C. She felt the only thing containing her fury was the need to comfort her children. Closing her eyes and taking a deep sigh she pulled her daughter to her in a big hug and assured her that everything would be ok. Inside C.C. was anything but sure of her convictions. Her youngest daughter ran over and hugged her mommy too.

"Just relax a while. I'll call you down for dinner."

After the talk with her daughter's, C.C. kept the conversations between her and her husband to almost nonexistent.

Don't I know you?

This day felt so strange from the moment she woke up. The alarm didn't go off and his car looked to be vandalized, so this meant C.C. would have to drive him to work. Before she dropped him off, the kids had to be brought to school first. They got to the school early because the girls had a meeting for their clubs.

When they pull up there's a few other cars letting students out as well. C.C. got out to escort her daughter's to their destinations. There is a car that pulls up beside her car. She sees Miss Hall getting out walking toward the entrance.

"Hey Annie!" the driver shouts.

She and C.C. both stop in their tracks. C.C.'s eyes widen and her mouth drops open. Miss Hall turns her head. The man is holding a bag up. She overhears the man say,

"You almost left your briefcase, Ann."

She didn't see the man's face because she was glaring at her husband who was gaping at the people standing next to their car. She finally turns to look at them herself and again is shocked to see Jesse standing by the driver's door.

"Well, good morning," Jesse says brightly.

Everyone's eyes seemed to be darting in every direction.

"Fancy meeting you here."

Jesse must have been the only one thinking nothing was wrong. C.C.'s husband glanced at Miss Hall then to her and cast his eyes down. Miss Hall's mouth shot open when she realized who was right beside her and cranes her neck between everyone. Suddenly, C.C. regained her voice.

"Good morning, Jesse. What are you doing here?"

"I'm dropping my fiancé off at work. This is such a coincidence!" He was smiling broadly at C.C.

Both his fiancé and her husband noticed this.

"You two know each other?" Miss Hall says sort of sourly.

C.C. narrows her eyes. Jesse answers,

"I'm publishing her book."

"Oh, so this is Jesse?" pipes up her husband. Suddenly by C.C.'s side as he looks from Jesse to Miss Hall, then finally back to C.C.

Jesse squints and says, "Yes. How are you?" Then he turns to face her husband and points saying, "You know you look familiar."

Miss Hall seems a bit anxious.

"Well ok. I'd better go before I'm late. I'll see you later."

"Yeah, we need to get going too."

Her husband chimes in and C.C. is still glaring at her husband.

"I guess he's right. It was nice to see you. I'll talk to you soon Jesse."

Everyone gets into their cars and begins to drive off. As they pass in the lot Jesse gives C.C. a bright smile and waves. C.C. gestures with her hand, 'I'll call you.'

Later that morning C.C.'s mind wouldn't stop racing. Too many bad and upsetting thoughts kept creeping up.

"I need to confront them, all of them."

She needed to speak to Jesse, but had no idea of exactly what to say to him. I mean how do you tell someone you suspect their fiancé of cheating? C.C. tried to occupy her thoughts by writing some new passages. She didn't want any reason to have to talk to her husband right now.

He came home early to deal with his car situation. He was getting a rental car while he repaired his. So, C.C. had the rest of the day to herself.

A friend of hers offered to keep the girls overnight for a sleepover. This was music to her ears. There was a long sigh. She heard him coming in the door. C.C. left everything on the table and got up to use the bathroom. It was about noon so she thought she'd fix some lunch as well. Anything to avoid her husband and the thoughts of his betrayal.

Adding fuel to the Fire

Feeling the stress build at home, Jesse just wanted to release his tension and concentrate on work. Do anything not to think about his issues. The day was filled with contacting authors to get approval on edited manuscripts. While looking through the manuscripts he realized that most of the things he was reading didn't hold much interest to him. This made him think of C.C. and how much her book's topic appealed.

Jesse tried to distract himself with lovely thoughts of tenderness and romance, but it was just that, a distraction from the real problem at hand. C.C was on his call list so he dialed anxiously anticipating her soothing voice. But when the call was answered, a man's voice responded gruffly.

Taken by surprise Jesse replied, "May I speak to C.C?"

"Who is this? What do you want?"

"My name is Jesse and..."

"Jesse!" he interrupted a little anxiously, "What do you want?" with a nervous quake in his voice.

"Um, yes. I am C.C's publisher."

There was a yell coming from the phone, Jesse waited and listened, then C.C. answered sweetly.

"Hello Jesse, I'm sorry about that. How are you?"

"Fine thanks."

"To what do I owe the pleasure?"

"Sadly I was calling about business, but it's always

a pleasure to hear your voice."

"Are you alright? I'm here if you need to talk."

"Oh C.C., I would love to, but I need to gather my thoughts right now." After a beat he says, "I love how soothing you can be."

"I could use some soothing myself," C.C. admitted sadly.

"Sounds like we both need a break," uttered Jesse.

"Would you like to have lunch with me?" C.C. secretly hoped he would agree.

"You know maybe if I eat I can clear the fog in my head."

Jesse agreed to meet up with C.C. a little later since they both had some free time.

They managed to do a little work over lunch, but each of them seemed so wound up. They were so used to being at ease in one another's company, yet their internal struggles weighed heavy today. The two decided to go to the nearby park. Jesse took the rest of the day off and C.C.'s daughter's had a play date, so they had time to relax a while longer.

"So, I know who my husband's having an affair with," C.C. stated rather casually.

Jesse looked shocked, but for some reason this perked him up.

"Really? How do you know that?"

"Well, my kids overheard him arguing and said a

name. Then I found her name and phone number. He doesn't know I suspect anything though. He has the nerve to try to keep my attention now. When I needed him, I was left lonely."

Jesse grabbed her hand and gently squeezed.

He whispered, "I'm paying attention," not realizing he said it out loud.

Shyly smiling C.C. replied, "I'm glad. That's enough about me, what's on your mind?"

Jesse slowly let go of her hand and takes a long sigh before saying,

"Well, I am supposed to be getting married; now we're having a baby, but I just feel like I'm not even involved. I'm still waiting to hear the results from the blood work I had done. We hardly even mention the baby at all!"

Jesse was becoming a little flustered now.

"Having a baby should be exciting. Things will get better, Jesse. They have to! Is there anything I can do for you?"

This time C.C. grabs his hand and smiles sadly at him.

"Come away with me," he says seriously.

She gapes at Jesse stunned, but without hesitation she responds,

"I don't think I can go away for long, but I can give you the night."

The two stared at one another and smiled. Silently, C.C. began to consider that being with him was wrong. After all, isn't this exactly what her husband has been doing to her...? Cheating? However, all they really wanted was to enjoy one another and get away from the chaos that was their life. They both had so much love to share and only wanted to have someone to return that love.

"Are you sure about this?" asked Jesse. Somehow reading her mind. He continued, "You understand me and make me feel good. I'd like to spend my time with you." "I wish I could give you all my time," he thought to himself.

The two have the entire evening together. It's always a joy to be in each other's company. They had so much to talk about. Laughter was infectious. The bad news C.C. wanted to tell Jesse about seemed to fade into the depths of her mind. Well, at least for now. She wanted the happiness to continue. The wariness within Jesse was being held at bay, briefly. Reality would be close again soon enough. Right now, nothing else mattered. Silently she thought to herself, "I don't want to be the one to tell him."

"Thank you for coming out with me," he said sincerely.

"Not at all. What would you like to do now, it's still early?"

"Can I stay the night with you? I just really don't want to go home and be alone," she said sadly.

There time is so special! Intimacy is their reason for meeting, it always rules out sex every time. Lord knows temptation plays a ruthless game against them though. But the longing looks, a gentle touch, soothing words and warm embraces calm the sexual beast yearning within both of them. Although this time the sexual desires are too hard to resist. This would lead up to their 'First Time'.

Calm before the Storm

After their first sexual encounter, C.C. got a glimpse of what it was to be with the genuinely romantic, passionate, kind man Jesse really was. She hadn't felt so wanton by anyone in a very long time and didn't want to lose the feeling. So there was no way she could tell Jesse what she knew, it would kill him! He would hate her for not telling him the truth.

Their getaway together was the only thing C.C. wanted to ponder. Bask in the memory of Jesse's smile and embrace. But the further they got to home the stronger the pain of hurting him with the secret she held ate away at her. They said their goodbyes once returning to their cars. Jesse gave her a big hug and C.C. began to cry. He asked what was wrong, but she just shook her head and kissed him softly on the lips.

Every moment that Jesse was on her mind stirred something within her that she couldn't escape. C.C. began to have intense heated dream unlike any other. With each night every time she closed her eyes she would envision this creature. Her pulse raced and the emotions were so real.

Waking Dream

I had a dream that frightened and thrilled me all at once.
There was a glimmer of you,
but the image would not come into focus.
I could sense your presence near to me.
I knew this to be you,
Although an uneasy chill in the atmosphere
made you seem a mystery.
I was used to the quivering I received with my thoughts of you,
However, a figure more intense stands before me radiating heat
and a carnal longing I have never seen.
This dream is the most intense I've ever known.
You were so domineering and commanding!
I could actually feel myself interacting with you.
The image is so vivid!
This can only be a dream.
The vision becomes clouded as confusion crosses my mind.
I know you don't feel this way, act this way.
Do you? Is this why the dream is frightening?
These sensations are what I wished you would feel
and show me in return.
Still I am scared.
On the other hand, could it be my nerves
anticipating reactions I so long for?
My breathing quickens and perspiration beads upon my
heaving breast.
As I toss and turn,

I reach out to grasp the familiar shape I know well.
I need to feel at ease.
Although your image is still hazy,
All at once, the forcefulness that seemed
unknowing becomes welcoming.
This can only be a dream. Yet I feel as if I were awake.
Nothing this fascinating can be so real!
My eyes open and begin to focus and the image now is clear.
It Is You… waking me from my dream!
What was a mystery now has been solved.
The carnal figure is you, longing to take me in reality.

With each of these waking dreams C.C. had to write them down as to remember the feeling and embrace the passion she encountered. But as she wrote and concentrated on what she was experiencing the anger involved with her husband set in more and more. She thought to herself: 'I only wanted a little attention, but he keeps brushing me off. Overtime hours keep him running out the door repeatedly, but now I find it wasn't work after all.

Trying to engage has become so hard. I wish he was even slightly interested in my book or anything I do. I once asked for an opinion on one of the entries but all I got was a shoulder shrug and an "It's alright." When I asked if there were any thoughts or feeling he told me, "Well, what do you expect me to say? I'm not into that girly stuff." She started to cry, although she wasn't sure if they were tears of anger or sorrow.

The Results

The two would not see each other again for a few days since their last meeting. The work on the book was at a standstill while going through publication, so there was no reason to call or see one another about work. However, the occasional text during the days keep them content and in contact with each other.

Because C.C. is fretting over this secret she holds, she decided to call Jesse to let him know. She didn't want him in the dark.

"It is always such a pleasure to hear your voice."

"Good morning Jesse." C.C. tried to keep her tone natural and calm as possible, but it would shutter through the words.

"I have something to tell you and I'm not sure how you're going to feel about it.

"Should I be worried?" Jesse couldn't think what this was about and felt a little concerned. "Well, I have a few meetings this morning. Would you like to come to my office later this afternoon?" He asked a little cautiously.

"Yes, that would be fine. Thank you."

Jesse heads to his first meeting once they hang up.

Just as Jesse was coming back to the office from his meeting a messenger was delivering a letter to him. He signs for it not really thinking much about it. But as he sat down at his desk, his mouth drops open. He was excited because he's been waiting for this a while. He simply wanted to read that everything was negative for anything being wrong with him and especially his unborn child. However, something had to be wrong here. He couldn't get passed the first lines of the report.

PATERNITY TEST: NEGATIVE. Jesse's eyes widened so far that his temples started to throb. Jesse blinked a couple of times, and then flipped the paper over to check if it was in fact his own name.

"What the hell is this? This is not supposed to be a paternity test and why in God's name is it negative?!"

Jesse continues to rant out loud to himself. The fury that was growing within him was frightening. He didn't know what to do first, call someone, leave or scream in anger. Deciding on the latter, Jesse slammed his hand down on the desk and knocked over everything in his path.

The knock on the door was tentative and went unanswered.

"LYING BITCH!"

Jesse screamed so loud the knocker opened the door and exclaimed shocked, "Jesse."

"What do you want? I didn't call for you!"

"I'm sorry."

Whirling around he said, "I want to be left alone."

Staring back at him was C.C.

"C.C., I thought you were my secretary."

"I'm sorry to bother you. You told me it was alright to come by." C.C. was already nervous to talk to Jesse, but now he was so upset, she really didn't think this was the right time.

With no preamble Jesse grabs C.C. up and kisses her hard. She pushes him off to catch a precious breath.

"What's the matter?"

"I need you." Jesse tried to kiss her again, but she raised her hands up in front of him.

"Stop. Talk to me."

She tried to implore him. Jesse began after a moment.

"She's been lying to me this whole time!"

"Lying about what?" she responded.

"It's not my baby." Jesse could barely speak the words. "I can't believe it's not my baby."

Putting her hands to her throat feeling like she'd choke, C.C. swallowed and replied,

"What do you mean? How do you know?"

Jesse turned around and picked up the piece of paper from the floor.

"Here, Read this."

She took it from him. Her hands began to shake. Everything was closing in on her and she didn't know how to react. Jesse was still fuming, but his anger ebbed slowly, noticing the stunned expression on C.C.'s face.

"I think I had the same reaction. I thought this was routine blood work, not a paternity test."

C.C. still remained silent.

"Are you ok? You seem more surprised than me."

He couldn't stop staring at her now and she couldn't turn her eyes from the report.

"I would love to know who the father is," Jesse says through gritted teeth.

C.C. finally looks up at Jesse and answers, "I believe I know."

"What? How would you know?"

C.C. hands back the piece of paper, takes a deep breath, then swallows. With her mouth going dry she blurts out, "My husband and your fiancé may be having an affair."

"What are you talking about? That's impossible."

"I know it may sound crazy, but there have been too many coincidences."

She was trying to explain, but without clarity.

"You're not making any sense C.C. They don't even know each other."

As he said this he became unsure.

"Her name is Annie isn't it?"

"Her name is Annette, but ...," stammering to get the words out, "I do call her Annie."

Feeling his anger resurface, Jesse questions C.C. "What's that got to do with anything?"

"I've noticed the two of them acting very peculiar

when we've been in the same vicinity. You know, since I found out she is my daughter's teacher."

"That doesn't mean anything."

"Do you remember I told you my kids heard him say the woman's name?"

She was trying to make him understand her assumptions, but C.C. could see Jesse's resistance to this news.

Jesse demands firmly, "What proof is that? I guess you assume it's the same person do you?"

As much as Jesse didn't like the relationship between he and his fiancé, be couldn't believe what C.C. was saying.

"You don't know what you're talking about!"

Jesse actually yelled at her. C.C. blinked very fast, taking a cautious step back. But she took a deep breath and retorted,

"I found her name on a card."

"That. Doesn't. Mean. Anything." He cut across her with a menacing tone.

C.C. raised her voice and said; "It had the time and date of their doctor's appointment!"

Spying his fear in his eyes she softens her voice and says,

"It was the same day you went to the doctor for the blood work."

Jesse's face went pale and he dropped himself in a nearby chair. There is silence in the office. With nothing much to say, after already saying so much, there was just silence.

C.C. came to kneel in front of Jesse. She took his face in her hands to make him look into her eyes. His were blank and void, but very sad.

"I'm sorry about this. Please don't be upset with me. I didn't know how to tell you."

"You mean you knew all along?" Jesse's eyes widened.

"No, I had my suspicions. But once you showed me the paternity test I knew it had to all be true. I was so scared to say anything. Scared that you'd hate me for telling you this." This was the last thing she wanted. Her feelings for him meant so much more than caring.

Jesse scooped C.C. up in his arms squeezing her tightly. This took her by surprise, but she reveled in the closeness she feared could have been lost. Jesse leaned back and gazed at her gliding his fingertips down her cheek.

He said, smiling, "Looks like we have more in common than we thought." She giggled. "I guess I should confront her about this fiasco."

"I hope I'm drawing the wrong conclusion here."

"Actually, I don't believe you are."

Suddenly he sat up straight. Something had come to him. A memory maybe. "I thought your husband was familiar when we met that day." It was C.C.'s turn to look confused. "He is the one I ran into the day I was going into the doctor's office."

"Oh my goodness! I do remember. I was on the phone with him when he said someone was in his way when he left the doctor's."

"Well, now what will we do? What's going to happen next?" C.C. said this out loud, whereas Jesse was thinking the same thing in his mind.

Several thoughts went through his mind now. The fiery anger he felt moments ago may have been calmed by C.C. but it certainly wasn't extinguished.

"How is it you can calm me even at a time like this?"

"I don't know really. I just do know I don't like to see you hurting."

C.C. was being so rational. He couldn't understand why she wasn't screaming with rage.

"What about you? This has got to be tearing you apart," he replies with concern in his voice. Hoping he could ease any pain she may be having. Surprisingly she admits to Jesse,

"Funny thing though, I don't think I love my husband enough anymore to really care. Sure I'm mad at his betrayal, but he's hurt me so often I've become numb to the heartache."

Just seeing C.C.'s reaction and hearing her speak with no regard to the fact that their significant others were involved was unbelievable. Jesse frowned at her.

"But aren't you a little angry?"

"Only for my children," she admitted sadly.

This statement weakened his heart a bit.

"Oh, I understand. Well, I am still furious! I can't believe I didn't realize any of this. But now I think I understand why she was rushing this damn wedding."

Jesse jumped up and started meticulously picking up everything he swiped off the desk. C.C. turned to help him and says,

"Are you alright?" Knowing the answer but still concerned. "I know you love her even though you've been unhappy." C.C. just couldn't say the name out loud, trying to keep her hateful feelings at bay.

"What do you want to do now?"

Jesse stops what he's doing. Takes a long sigh and breathes, "I just don't know. This really hurts. How could she do this to me?"

"Jesse, didn't we just do the same thing? Cheat on them."

"But you know it's not the same. The two of them had to be seeing each other for some time."

"That doesn't excuse what we've done."

"But C.C., we never actually had sex and she is pregnant!" Jesse raised his voice and C.C. blanched.

"I know it wasn't penetration, but for us it was more emotionally charged and sometimes that's just as bad."

Silence stretched between them.

"I know he hasn't really loved me for a while. Well, not like he used to anyway. But you..."

"Yes me, I stupidly love her. I thought she loved me in return. When she stopped showing and then stopped telling me, I should have sensed it."

C.C. walks closer to Jesse, reaches for him and smoothes her fingertips down his cheek. Jesse closed his eyes and grabbed her hand in his. He simply whispered,

"Thank you, my love."

This surprised C.C. greatly. She blinked and said,

"So what are you going to do?"

"I guess I'll have to confront all these issues. Just wished she loved me."

"I'm sure she does."

"This is how she chose to make me believe that."

"So I guess the question still remains, what do you want to do?" C.C. stated very seriously.

"Jesse, will you stay with her now that you know?"

Shocked by her question he opened his mouth as if to speak but quickly closed it. When he does answer his confusion is evident.

"I truly don't know. Will you stay with your husband?"

"My decision is a little easier because I've grown out of love some time ago. I think we're going through the motions for the kids. So no, I may not stay. Whereas you, you need to decide if you're still in love with her and are her acts forgivable." C.C. paused, waiting to see if he would answer. "Do you still love her?"

"Yes."

"Are you still in love with her, Jesse?"

Jesse's eyes widened, but he stares intently at C.C.

He closes his eyes for a moment; he opens them and says quietly,

"I think I'm falling in love with you, C.C."

She gives him a shy smile. Just as she began to respond Jesse's office phone rang. They both turn their heads toward it.

"I'll let you get that."

"No, please don't go."

"It's ok. I have to pick up the kids."

C.C. frowns at the thought of possibly running into Jesse's fiancé. The woman who could be having her husband's child. This made Jesse frown as well, clearly reading her expression. He picked up the phone and placed the call on hold. He suddenly grabbed C.C. into a bone crushing hug.

"I'll talk to you soon."

She walked towards the door.

"C.C.," he called to her. "I'm sorry."

She turned back to gaze at Jesse and responds, "So am I."

Let's Talk

Both C.C. and Jesse had such heartache weighing on them. For C.C. this news just fueled her mission to make her life her own and continue to care for her children without contempt. She already felt her marriage falling apart. This just sealed it. Her only regret would be the turmoil that their daughters may experience.

But of course Jesse had to decide whether to end the life he hadn't really started. The woman he planned to spend his life with has began a life all her own. How could he live with her knowing everything was a lie? He gave his all in the belief that they had a lasting love. A love that is full of passion, intimacy and trust. He now saw that he surely lost these things in his fiancé, but also saw that he found these desired traits in C.C.

The two of them dreaded the conversations that lay in wait. What would be the best way to approach this situation? What if the suspicions are wrong? But they couldn't be, too many things were coming in line.

Later this day C.C. went on like any other. Picking

up her children, going home to start dinner, and cleaning up a little before setting down for the evening waiting for her husband to show up at home. She heard the door open and turned to see him come in. He was so surprised to see her staring.

"Hello, C.C." He paused as she just stared.

"Hello," she responded and got up to go to the kitchen and took a plate out for him. "Your dinner is here if you want it."

"Oh, thank you. Where are the girls? Have they eaten already or you?"

"Yes. I told them to get cleaned up and they'd see you later if you were coming home."

"What do you mean, if? Of course I was coming home."

"I can't imagine why?" she mumbles and turns to face her husband and he stares with his mouth open, then simply shrugs and walks away.

"C.C. come back here." He starts to yell, but when she snaps her neck to face him again, the menacing glare takes him by surprise. He blinks a couple of times then lowers his voice and says, "C.C. please, come back. Talk to me."

"What could you possibly have to say to me?"

"Well… I just thought…"

"Well, how about you start with how you are going to be a father." He continues to gape at her.

"What are you talking about?" He finally manages to find his.

"Don't pretend you don't know what I'm talking about." She rolls her eyes and puts her hands on her hips. "Come on let it out. And don't even try to lie," she demands. "And before you say another word I know about you and Annie." She says her name with such disdain, but never raises her voice. His eyes look to well up with tears, but collecting himself he begins to step toward C.C. She steps back from his reach.

"Don't touch me! It's too late for that. Just talk to me because I have nothing left to say." He sighs long and swipes his hands over his face.

"Would you like to sit down?" She just crosses her arms and leans against the wall. After a beat he sits himself down to face her and fiddles with his fingers. "Ok C.C. I won't hide anymore. I was having an affair, but that's all over." When she has no comment he continues. "We did meet up at the girls' school, but we knew each other years ago and reconnected."

C.C. comes to sit on the opposite side of her husband and stares at him with tears in her own eyes.

"Why?"

"Why, what?"

"Why don't you love me?"

"C.C. I do love you."

"Don't say that. You haven't loved me for a long time."

He bows his head and whispers, "I've been so selfish."

"And self absorbed and heartless," C.C. chokes out

with her tears streaming now.

"C.C., how do you know about the baby?"

"Jesse showed me his results and they were negative." He looks at her confused and then frowns. "Yeah, you remember Jesse, Annie's fiancé?" She wipes her tears away and gets up to walk around.

"Oh, right, your publisher. Why would he tell you about something so private?"

"Because I went to tell him my suspicions."

"I didn't realize you two were so close." His tone is accusatory. She stops in front of him.

"Don't you dare!" Looking for the right words to say to him without losing control ~ it all comes to a head…

How Dare You

How dare you treat me this way?
Mean and hurting actions set upon me.
I thought I knew you, but I don't recognize this strange,
This unknown creature staring me down
with darkness in their eyes
Holding my breath as a shield anticipating the blow
I'm not sure will come.
Who is this stranger?
I open my mouth to question my fear and then struck down
with words so forceful physical pain could not be much worse.
Hurtful, Degrading, Disgusting things replied to the confused

look on my face.
Confused that you could be so uncaring.
How dare you say these things to me?
Gasping for air from shock…BAM!
Whipping my neck around in disbelief, I place my hands over my face as the pain sets in.
Questioning fear vastly becoming understandable anger!
Dazed, I rise to my feel to better to view my attacker.
I don't know this stranger!
How dare you give me this pain?
Hit in my face ~ How dare you make me cry?
I am not a stranger to you! Some random enemy, come to battle!
[Did I do something to deserve this?] No, I didn't deserve to be brought to my knees!
Hatred and violence stands before me glaring with unforgiving rage. The darkness consumes this stranger concealing my tearful presentation.
Yelling – Screaming – Thrashing about –
He's racing toward me as I cower into hiding.
He should not be so scary!
Now the anger in me is climbing! He has no right to treat me this way. I must get away from this strange creature of darkness. Never again can I endure such hurt. I will not allow this pain to take me down.
I wipe away the tears, plant my feet firmly on the ground.
Gaining my composure and taking a steadying breath, I raise my hand in defense and find my superior voice:

HOW DARE YOU!

Back away from me stranger, I do not know who you are! You would not have found the words to tear me apart or find the strength to knock me down. You could never have known me! Not doing what you do to expose my tears and cause me disgust. How dare you make me fear my love and question my trust in another!

You are a stranger to me!

"I've put up with all your abuse, neglect and heartache for a very long time now. No more!"

He sits with his eyes opened wide in shock. He reaches up to grab her arms to make her stop.

"Please, forgive me. Sit down." Reluctantly she sits beside him.

"You know your children think you don't love them? They've overheard some of your conversations."

He leans back and puts his hands through his hair. "Of course I love them, they are my heart." Swallowing, he adds, "I guess this is why she's been acting out?" The shame and guilt shows in his face.

"We will have to talk to the girls together at some point. Things cannot keep going on this way. For any of us." C.C appeals sadly to her husband. He looks up into C.C.'s eyes and sees the hurt behind them. Reaching out to her, he strokes her cheek. But without realizing it she leans into his gentle touch.

"C.C., I'm sorry. I never meant to hurt you. I've been selfish and I know you must hate me."

"Oh, Dear, I don't think I hate you, just disappointed in you. I hoped things could be better between us, but we've grown apart and I'm ok with that." He looks mournful at her words and lowers his gaze.

"So you don't love me anymore."

"I will always love you. We share a bond that can never be broken…" he smiles brightly at the thought "… our girls." The smile descends and he runs his hands through his hair. "But you must know I'm no longer in love with you."

"Yes, I know I don't deserve your love, but I hoped."

They sit and smile at each other then start to snicker. The air seemed to be very light between C.C. and her husband. They both were waiting for an ultimate fight, but each knew that their relationship as a couple was over and yelling and screaming was pointless. Quite soon, understanding that there was no pressure of satisfying the other, they began to relax with each other. The two reminisced a bit. This was brought on mostly by her husband. C.C. enjoyed the conversation simply because it's what she missed from him all this time.

After a long sigh he asks, "Where do we go from here?"

She pauses before answering, "We need to consider what's best for the children. Although we can't keep living a lie, they won't be happy if we aren't happy."

He replied, "What would make you happy C.C.?"

"To be understood, wanted, and appreciated. Mostly I want love. To be loved. To be able to love myself." As she halts her words to him she inwardly realizes what she really needs…

Acceptance of Self

Trying to keep my cool while, everything feels that it's crumbling down around me! I work hard to make things happen, but like throws obstacles in my path daily. I steer clear, but I can't get around them. Feeling useless and worthless, tearing down my defenses, but keeping mindful of my determination. It is so hard being an adult!

Responsibility is a hard task to take on, full of pressure as well as dedication. Wishing things would come a little easier instead of one-step forward then two steps back. Still keeping my cool, but breathing shallow breathes. Holding in painful tears to make others at ease.

I'm shouting inside, beating myself up criticizing every decision gone a rye. I have no one to blame but myself. All of my suffering, maybe I don't work hard enough? Maybe I don't deserve success or happiness.

I just want better. I want to feel useful.
I want to be recognized as an adult.
I WANT MORE!

More than the minimum! More than OK! More out of life! Satisfaction is what I want. I understand and it has come to me that my hurt, my fear, & my tears will cease with my Satisfaction. Satisfaction in a job well done. Satisfaction in my abilities. Satisfaction in myself.

I am an adult and in control of my emotions!
No matter how low or lost these emotions bring me down, they cannot keep me down. As an adult, I have learned to get up, because the walls that are crumbling can be rebuilt.
The obstacles in the way can be diverted.
The scrutiny can be ignored.
Moreover, the tears from all the unwanted emotions can be wiped away.
I am Satisfied.
I kept my cool!

As she says the words her thoughts automatically go to Jesse. Knowing how caring and gentle a man he is makes her face glow with pleasure. She thinks to herself, 'Jesse makes me happy!' In looking at her face he can see her whole attitude has changed.

"What is it?" he says concerned.

"Well, you were right when you said me and Jesse were close. Next to bringing my book to life, we have been comforting one another." The man's face is ashen.

"You mean you've cheated on me." He whispers this in total disbelief. In a million years he would never think this possible.

C.C. stares and purses her lips and raised an eye-brow. She answers, "To some extinct yes. We found comfort when we know we lost it." The shame crept back across his face.

"So I guess he's what you want."

"He's shown me what I want." He simply gawks at C.C. not quite understanding. C.C. just shakes her head clearly noticing his confusion. All she could think was 'He really doesn't know me at all.'

He stands up and walks to the kitchen for a drink. She turns in the seat when he offers her one in return. "Thank you." With a head nod he takes his seat next to her again.

Feeling her mouth dry, she takes a sip, swallows and says, "I know we have a lot to work out, but what will you do about your baby?"

This topic is not one she wanted to explore. It's the main cause of her hurt in this scandal. How could he ignore their children then turn around and knock up some random woman?!

Nervousness began to set in as she waited for what she thought was to be his answer. Surely he wanted to leave and be with the new family he created. He gets up again saying nothing. Walks to his jacket and pulls out an envelope. C.C. follows him with her eyes still waiting for a response. He opens the letter and hands it to her. As she reads her eyes expand and she covers her mouth with her hand in shock.

"I am as surprised as you. If that were possible," noticing her stunned expression.

As the words are able to form in her mind again she becomes confused. "What is this? I thought… I just assumed…"

"Of course I knew there was a chance, but when I saw it read negative I thought I was off the hook, but then you said Jesse's test was negative as well… I don't know what I thought really."

"Oh my goodness!" She begins to tear up once more.

Exasperated he huffs, "What's wrong? Now we don't have anything to worry about."

"Poor Jesse. This is going to kill him even more. My poor Jesse." She places her hand on her heart. Her husband frowns at this gesture.

"I thought you might be glad I wasn't that baby's father." She looks at him and furrows her brow.

"This doesn't change anything for us. And the only reason I'm not throwing you out is because of our children and because I know we need to come to some sort of arrangement."

He says, "So you feel you need to 'comfort' him now?"

"I want to comfort him," she says without batting an eye.

"You would leave me for him?"

"I would leave you for me. It's just that now I know I can."

"Does this mean we are officially over?"

She reaches up to graze his cheek and sadly whispers, "I'm afraid it is." They both stare into each other's eyes. He grabs her hand to caress it then pulls C.C. in a powerful embrace. Surprisingly she doesn't stop him and wraps both arms around his neck.

"We will work it out," she whispers. "Let's go to bed now."

He leans back with a raised eyebrow. "Should I sleep on the couch?"

With a slight pause she answers, "No."

C.C. turns to walk away. All the while thinking, 'We've been sleeping together, not really as husband and wife, one more night won't kill me.' He watches her leave the room with a smile and sigh of relief.

"I'll just check on the girls before I come up." When she doesn't turn back or respond his smile fades and shrugs his shoulders.

This day was so draining. The minute C.C. walked to her room the tears began to fall. She tried so hard not to let him see the hurt she was really feeling. Suddenly her phone rings making her jump. It's Jesse. Why is he calling at this hour? Something must be wrong. Answering the phone she closes her eyes and says, "Jesse, how are you?"

"I was wondering the same about you."

"Oh I'll be fine. We talked and we're going to work through some things before any decisions are made. But I'm ok."

C.C. can hear her husband in the hall. "Where are you?"

"Well I'm staying out for the evening. I just can't go home."

"Have you talked to Annie yet?" She could hear someone at the door, but no one enters.

"No, not yet. I can't face her right now," he murmurs wearily.

"Oh Jesse, this whole situation is enough for anyone to bear. I've heard so much information, some you won't believe."

"Do you want to talk about it?"

"Sweetie, I don't think you want to hear anymore tonight."

"Maybe you're right. But for tonight I would like to see you."

"I'd love to see you too. But for tonight I need to be home." While finishing up the call she hears her husband clear his throat outside the door. "Jesse, I'm going to say goodnight." He walks in the room. "I'll call you later," she replies and hangs up the phone.

"Did I disturb you?"

"No, it's ok."

"I spoke with the girls briefly. They're sleeping now."

They dress for bed and lie down in silence. In the quiet darkness C.C. begins to whimper again. He turns and runs his hand down smoothing her hair then rubs her back. This makes C.C. cry even harder. Moving closer to her he snakes his arm around her pulling her to face him.

"C.C. I'm sorry about everything." She squeezes her eyes shut. Just then he leans in and kisses her lips softly. Through the tears she opens her eyes shocked.

"What are you doing?"

"Let me comfort you."

She closes her eyes and cries harder, then grabs his face down to meet her lips once more. She continues to cry as he continues to kiss her, but she makes no moves to stop him. This is what she's wanted from him all the long. To be gentle and passionate and want only her. She began to caress his body in return and her cries slowly ebb as she accepts him into her. He looks down into her eyes and wipes a stray tear from her face.

"Are you alright?" he asks soothingly.

"Just kiss me." Not wanting to talk anymore, only revel in this simple pleasure of easing her pain with her husband, at least for a little while.

He reins kisses all over her body, both tuning everything else out. Nothing mattered but them two. Although both were quietly thinking this would be the last time they would share this closeness. They begin to feel their bodies quicken and he suddenly rolls over holding C.C. in his arms to a sitting position.

Rocking back and forth with their arms wrapped around tightly, he looks into her eyes and says, "Please don't cry anymore. I never want to hurt you again."

"Hold me close. I need this." He complies and they explode in each other's arms like they never have before. Now they both have tears in their eyes. Falling back onto the bed they spoon and quickly fall fast asleep.

As the morning approached so did C.C. She opens her eyes and feels an arm draped across her. C.C. easily eases out of bed to shower and get ready to proceed with the day at hand. But not before she reflects on the previous nights events.

"Good morning." C.C. hears him behind her.

"I hope it will be." She turns to face him. "We need to talk to the girls…soon."

Sighing heavily he replies, "I guess you're right." He so hoped their connection last night would somehow rekindle them.

Lightning Strikes

That night after speaking to C.C., Jesse was able to rest just enough to put his head to the pillow. He knew the coming day was going to be unbearable.

Jesse woke hesitantly the next morning dreading the confrontation that must take place with his fiancé. The anguish he felt through this situation was confusing him. His mind was telling him to be angry, but his heart was in conflict over the deceit of his fiancé and the overwhelming joy he received from C.C. that seemed to dull the pain.

Trying to shake it off, Jesse takes a cleansing shower and prepares to leave for another work day. But before he collects his belongings he decides not to check out of the room, just in case.

When arriving to work he asks his secretary not to disturb him just as she hands over all the messages he received as he enters the office. They're mostly business related, but several are from his fiancé seeming very upset or concerned at where he is. Reading through the messages the anxiety was building. He couldn't avoid the issues much longer.

It's still early so Jesse figured he'd get the important work matters cleared away and clear his mind a little in the process. The more pressing situations at home would need his full attention.

It's about lunch time and all Jesse wants is to hide. The hunger pangs are starting to set in. His nerves probably wouldn't allow anything to stay down anyway. But he needed to keep his strength up so he decided to order in lunch. He reaches for the phone, but the line is open.

"Hello. Is someone there?"

"Hello Jesse." He lets out a sigh of relief and his spirits lift, but only slightly.

"Oh C.C., I'm glad you called. I feel like I'm losing my mind. I have no idea what I'm feeling right now."

"Have you talked yet?"

"No. I think I'm procrastinating because I really don't know what to say to her."

"Maybe once you deal with all of this, things will become clear. I know it did for me," she says lowering her voice.

Hesitantly Jesse asked, "Did he tell you what was going on? Were all your assumptions correct?"

"Yes. Mostly. But also no." There was silence for a few seconds.

"I don't understand."

"I found out a lot, but one thing I felt I should warn you about." C.C. was nervous to say anything in fear of what Jesse might do when he heard. As he listened to these words a cold shiver crept across him.

"Warn me? What could you need to warn me about?"

"Um, I saw my husband's paternity test too and it was negative as well." The phone seemed to go dead. As C.C. was waiting for some sort of response she could hear a low whimper coming through the line. "Jesse did you hear me?"

"Yes."

"Are you alright?" She regretted the question as it spilled out of her mouth.

"How would you expect me to feel?" C.C. didn't really know what to say to that, but tried just the same.

"Maybe there's an explanation. I'm not sure what, but you never know."

With a huff he starts, "Are you serious? What's with you pleading her case?"

"Oh no, that's not it at all. But I think you need to hear her out to get the whole story."

"C.C. forgive me if this seems harsh, but just because your marriage is over doesn't mean everyone else has it all figured out."

She gasps in shock with slight annoyance. "Jesse I was only trying to ease your mind a little so you don't blow up unnecessarily. After all there is blame to share in this horrible ordeal. Don't forget our part." Her tone is horse with an edge to it. The phone goes silent again. When neither can take it any longer Jesse speaks up quickly.

"Oh C.C. please forgive me. I hate what this is doing to me. I never want to hurt you. I don't want to hurt anyone. It's just that I am hurting so much." His voice is almost a whimper.

"We're all under a lot of pressure. I'm going to let you go so you don't have any more distractions."

"But I need you C.C." Jesse whispers softly and C.C. gasps. This is what she secretly hoped for, but knew it couldn't be admitted to. Not now when things were so complicated.

"Jesse you need to finish this. I mean work through this." She becomes nervous wondering if he picked up on her reference.

"I know you're right. And I will handle this." There is a long sigh between them both. Even on the phone in silence so much is being said.

"Goodbye Jesse."

"Goodbye C.C. Oh by the way. I am proud to say, you're book is completed." He hangs up and C.C. begins to cry. All of her emotions were boiling over.

I Didn't Realize

After so much time was spent chasing a dream,
Why was it so easy to let the dream fade?
It took so long to get together.
Once we did, you wanted to get away.
We were all either of us needed at the time,

but I think I was foolin' myself.
I lived each day to be with you,
but with me isn't where you wanted to be.
My love was waiting for you.
You just never came to claim it.
I thought I was enough, but you seemed to need more.
How is it you would proclaim true feelings, yet never say that something was missing?
What was lacking your satisfaction?
Where would improvements need to be placed?
You were nowhere to be found, although
I did not know you were lost.
You disappeared right from under my nose and I never even took my eyes off you.
How is it that I lost track of such a gem…
A gem that meant the world to me.
I learned it was never mine alone to treasure.
I loved you enough to let you go,
'Cause it's so easy to come back to you.
I wanted only to run to you.
But all I do is cry when near to you.

As the evening comes to an end and Jesse heads home, anxiety, along with uncertainty, hovers over him. Walking into the apartment he doesn't know what to expect. Not coming home last night was supposed to calm him before attempting to confront his fiancé, but now that he's back here and sees her standing there waiting the calm he's held on to is now tentative. He's not sure what to do first as he looks at her.

"Jesse! Where have you been?"

"Contemplating," he says dryly.

"Contemplating about what? Why didn't you call me?" Jesse continues into the room and lays his bags down. Taking off his jacket he turns back in front of her. She stands stock still and stares with tears in her eyes.

"Annie, do you love me?"

Her eyes widen slightly as she answers, "Yes."

He closes his eyes and sighs deeply before he asks, "How would I know that?"

Annie blinks several times and gasps. With a stutter she replies, "How can you ask me that?"

"Because I want an answer," he begins through gritted teeth. "You owe me the truth." Her mouth falls open and the shock of this statement halts all sound. She has never heard Jesse speak in this manner before. When she doesn't respond right away, Jesse steps back from her and drops his head.

Not understanding what's going on and fearing him walking away from her, she reaches out to grab his arm and says, "Jesse, what's this about? What truth are you talking about?"

He steps toward his bag and pulls out the envelope containing the paternity results. As she aims to take it from his hand she notices Jesse is shaking. "What's this?" she asks with a trembling voice.

"It's the truth!"

Confusion and apprehension cover her face. Glancing up into Jesse's eyes she opens the envelope and takes out the paper. Jesse's fists are clenched by his sides. Annie's hand flies to cover her mouth and the tears now full blown sobs. Her hand quickly drops to the little bump at her stomach, then she falls down to the nearest seat. Looking down at her weeping figure is all the truth he needs.

The rage he's been concealing is overflowing. As he runs his hands through his hair he hollers, "I loved you! How could you do this to me? To us?"

She pauses in her crying and chokes out, "Loved? You loved me?" And then the tears continue.

"Well this whole negative paternity test is certainly making me question my feeling as well as your feelings for me." Jesse's voice is loud, but full of unshed tears.

"Jesse I don't understand wh…"

"YOU CHEATED ON ME! What don't you understand? Because I understand perfectly that you've been playing me through this whole time. Rushing this sham of a wedding, just so you would have an automatic father for your baby." He can't keep the bitterness from his rampage.

She has lost all ability to speak. Her eyes are full of everything she can't say. "What? How… how could this be?"

He answers her, "Well it's a funny thing, when you're having an affair with a married man there tends to be some risk involved." His sarcastic words make her cry even harder but confusion is also coming across her mind.

"Jesse, No. This can't be right!" Annie holds the paper in her hands looking at it carefully. She throws it to the floor and reaches for Jesse but he stops her hands from touching him. "Jesse please listen to me it's got to be wrong. Look it could be that it's too early and we need to do it again."

"We weren't supposed to do it at all Annette!" He yells so loud that she flinches and backs away. He goes on in a fury. "I guess you're going to say this other guy's test is right since it's also negative."

"You don't know what you're saying. There's no way you would know something like that." She tries to ease her breathing and dash some of the tears away, but what he says next breaks her even further.

"His wife told me everything and he admitted the truth about you two including the paternity test results." Tears begin to well up in Jesse's eyes again. He moves closer to her and her eyes are bulging from their sockets. He grabs her by the arms and almost shakes her as he says, "Why?!"

She just keeps shaking her head and muttering, "No, this isn't how I wanted you to find out."

"Don't you mean you didn't want me to find out?"

"I'm sorry Jesse," she says through her sobs.

"Tell me how long," he whispers under his breath. Looking at her now seemed to resurrect C.C.'s earlier words. 'Hear her out.' So that's what he wanted, to hear her talk. He wanted to give her the chance to explain, if that were even possible. But he was beginning to calm, only just. Of course he felt he had every right to be furious at her betrayal, but he has some blame in this tale.

As she tries to pull herself together she gazes at Jesse with a pleading stare. "We've known each other since high school and we reconnected at a reunion. We both had too much to drink and it started from there." She stops to see if he would respond, but he simply glared and waited for her to continue. "We were getting really close… I was so weak Jesse." The tears start again as she realizes he has no comment.

Suddenly he replies, "You thought you would trap me into marrying you and raising another's baby?"

"No! I wanted to marry you."

"No, what you wanted was to have your cake and eat it too. And it seems like you wanted even more than cake, because neither one of us is the father." He redirects so coldly. She stands with her jaw dropped in horror.

"Jesse, what are you implying?"

"Well, when two paternity tests are negative there must be a third option." Disdain drips from every word. His pain is more evident now.

"There hasn't been anyone else!"

"Just this married man."

She lowers her head and her voice saying, "Yes."

Jesse starts to walk away. "Something has to be wrong about the test."

"Which one are you saying has to be wrong," he exclaims with an annoyed sigh. She's taken aback and shutters a reply.

"Um, I wish it was yours, but maybe both tests were tainted. It has to be," she whispers again.

Annie holds her head in her hands feeling the embarrassment of the situation. But she softly cries as she rubs her palms across her abdomen. Jesse watches the scene in confusion. His anger is palpable; although this is the woman he loved and planned to spend the rest of his life with.

It's quiet in the room. Seeing Annie cooing and murmuring to herself, all he wants to do is hold her. Comfort her. He hasn't seen her show this much emotion in a long time. He begins to move next to her, but slightly pauses realizing that this is why he's become so attracted to C.C. It all made him remember that he and C.C. have become just as intimate. His hurt was blinding him to the fact that he pursued this relationship not just because something was lacking in their home, but he actually wanted to be with C.C.

The hardship and misunderstandings with Annie was just an excuse. When Jesse makes to sit next to her he hears her whisper, "You don't deserve this," as she continues to caress her belly. He slides his arm across her shoulder and she is startled. Turning to look at him she utters, "Please forgive me. I never meant for this to happen."

"Nobody ever means to break someone's heart, but that's what being selfish gets us." His words seem to be harsh but the tone he uses is anything but. Annie glances up at Jesse and tears flow freely. He pulls her to him and holds her firmly as she whimpers in his arms. Suddenly Jesse's body is trembling and he squeezes her tighter. She tries to lean back.

"Jesse, are you alright?" When looking into his face he also has tears.

"No Annie. I'm not."

"Why are you trembling?"

"I'm scared," he says closing his eyes.

She blinks unsure and asks, "What do you have to be scared of?"

"I've never felt this way before." He hesitates, looking for the right way to express his thoughts.

"You hate me now don't you?"

"Yes. And I don't like it. However, I still love you. I will always love you." She smiles at these words and reaches to touch his cheek. He grabs her hand pressing a gentle kiss to it. "But I'm scared. I'm scared I'm no longer in love with you."

She drops her hand from his and tries to speak but he places a finger to her lips halting her words.

"Please Ann, let me say this. I don't like this, any of it."

"Jesse, Please. Can't we…"

"No. I need to tell you this before I lose my nerve."

Taking a deep breath he resumes. "I thought I was all you needed or wanted. But somewhere I started to notice that you were slowly forgetting about me."

"No, that's not true. I never…"

"When did you first realize you loved me?" She stared unsure. When she doesn't answer he says, "Exactly what I mean. You can't recall any events that we've shared. Like the restaurant." She hangs her head down. "I never once assumed you were seeing someone else. Let alone sleeping with them. Then you end up pregnant. This is not the way I planned on starting our life!"

He stands to walk around the room as frustration comes over him. His temper must remain calm in order to do this. "As much as I'd like to place all the blame on you for coming between what we had, it's just not the case."

"What do you mean, Jesse?" realization dawning. "Where were you last night? Were you alone?" she asks cautiously. He narrows his eyes slightly before responding.

"Yes I was alone, but I didn't want to be."

Scared of the answer he might give, she meekly asks, "Who did you want?"

Jesse takes a moment, closes his eyes and he can visualize her face. Before he opens them he replies, "C.C." He opens to look on her.

The reaction is expected. Sheer shock! The shock doesn't first seem to register on the name, but on the fact there was in fact a name. However, as the revelation processed further everything came clear to her.

"Wait a minute. C.C.? You mean his wife?" He simply nods in agreement. "And she's the one who told you all of this too." She snickers to herself. "I didn't even know about the results before her it seems and I'm the one having the baby." Annie's voice is more agitated at this thought.

Jesse can see the expression of annoyance on her face. He shakes his head and frowns knowing that she does it when all matters don't involve her and her needs. This feeling alone was one Jesse was beginning to realize more than he cared to admit.

"You know, I always knew you were a little spoiled, but now I'm starting to understand just how selfish you are."

"What? How dare you!"

"You don't stop to think what your actions do to anyone else. You're only worrying about your own feelings. And not this chaos you've caused."

She stares dumbfounded for a second, then seems to gain her confidence and counters. "Well it appears that you were busy being selfish in what you wanted too. Just what exactly have you been doing with that woman behind my back?"

His look of loathing at this question referring to C.C. was almost violent. He had to take a step back away from her to control the emotion rising. He answers her, "Up until very recently, we've done nothing but talk about work. She is very professional that way. Then when we weren't laughing and sharing interests, we were a shoulder to cry on. She is extremely caring that way. We also comfort each other in ways I never hoped for. She is exceptionally passionate in that way." He stops his explanation and takes a deep breath.

The words are actually just sinking into his mind. Throughout his confession he imagined C.C.'s face. Her smooth voice. Her gentle touch. Then the sensation of her soft kiss pressing his lips. Completely tuning all else out. But focusing back to the here and now seeing Annie's face, he shakes it off. She is awe struck and dismayed and again she is clutching her belly.

"You love her, don't you?" she cries as her voice reappears. He doesn't answer right away but takes the time to consider her words. He knows he has strong feelings for C.C. and they could be love, but is it real or is he merely displacing his resentment of one for the compassion of another?

Contemplating his true feelings, he didn't dare speak them aloud. Not now. Not to her. Almost defensive he answers, "What difference does it make? She means nothing to you, so why concern yourself?"

"I had hoped there was still a chance to work things out with us," she says sadly.

"How could I stay with you knowing you carry another man's child?"

"This has to be your child! We will retake the test

and then we will be sure. We'll get through this Jesse. It's over between me and him." She speaks at a rush trying to get his full attention. "Please Jesse. I need you now."

This one statement makes him listen. He asks her, "What precisely do you need me for?"

"I want you to stay with me."

"But you don't need me and that's the problem," he states mournfully.

"What about our wedding?"

"There is no way I can marry you now. I started having doubts even before I found out you were cheating on me."

"But Jesse I love you. You can't do this."

"I love you too, but I am not in love with you. Not anymore." As Jesse allowed the words to be spoken he understood what that meant. He knew without a doubt what he wanted to do. What he needed to do to make him happy. And what he needed to be happy was C.C. There was no denying this anymore.

Annie starts to shiver. She gets up to her feet and almost collapses back down. Staggering she walks closer to Jesse. "No Please. You don't know what you're saying. Please…Oww!"

He peers down to her a little worried. "What's wrong?"

"Nothing. Jesse we can work this out. Work on us." She grabs her stomach again. This time she falls back to a chair.

"Annie I don't want to have to work on us. I don't think we should have to. There's so much that's different between us. Even after all this time."

He watches her sitting there quivering now so he kneels in front of her. Just as he goes to speak, he notices sweat beads forming on her forehead. He believes she's only reacting to what he's told her. But when she crumbles down to her knees he can see something is wrong,

"Annie, talk to me! What are you doing? Are you alright?!"

"It hurts," she whimpers. "I can't breathe, Jesse. Please help me."

She is crying now. Jesse is scared and doesn't know what to do. She's lying on the floor shaking ferociously. He jumps up to run to the phone. He calls 911. "I need an ambulance right away! My fiancé is in excruciating pain. She's pregnant. Please… Yes… Quickly!"

After hanging up he returns to her covering her with a blanket. "Oww…Ohh, my stomach hurts so much. What is this?" They both are on the floor, fear surrounding them.

"I don't know Annie. The ambulance is coming. I'm sorry. I don't know what to do." He has tears in his eyes as well. "I'm right here." He holds on to her hand tightly.

Suddenly the door bell rings and he flings the door open. Everything happens in a flash. The paramedics try to turn her to assess the problem, but she won't release the tight ball she's wound in. When they manage to lift her, her breathing is shallow. She's placed on a stretcher. Jesse looks down and sees blood everywhere.

"What's this? She's bleeding!"

The paramedics continue to move quickly. "You say she's pregnant?" Jesse nods rapidly. "We need to move. You can ride with or follow behind us. But we need to go." Remaining calm, they continue on outside to the ambulance.

"Jesse I need you." Annie's voice is strangled. He jumps in and they're off.

Pain

Waiting in the waiting room with no clue to what's happening is torture. He keeps seeing the anguish in her eyes and that blood. Pacing back and forth he can't imagine her in this kind of agony. He needed to do something. Be with her. She needed him now. How could he have spoken to her like that? He did love her, care for her. As much as he hated what she did, he could never hate her. He couldn't just sit here doing nothing. So he takes out the phone. Family. Her family needed to know. They should be here too. The calls are made. Now wait some more.

Once Jesse put the phone away the alarm sounded from his pocket. He was scheduled to see C.C. about marketing strategies later that morning. He couldn't leave now. Not without knowing what's going on. He scrolls to C.C.'s number.

"Hello. Good morning," she says sleepily.

"Hello C.C. Sorry to call so early, but something's happened and I won't be able to make our meeting."

"Is everything alright?"

"I don't know yet."

"Jesse you're scaring me. Where are you?"

"At the hospital." His responses are becoming clipped.

"Hospital? Why?"

"Blood. So much blood."

"Jesse what happened?!"

"She was in pain and I couldn't help her. She kept grabbing her stomach."

"Oh my goodness. Jesse she may be having a miscarriage."

"Is that really so painful," he asks really worried.

"It can be very severe. It depends."

"Annette Hall." A doctor comes out to speak to Jesse.

"C.C. I got to go. I'm sorry." He hangs up the call. "Yes doctor. Please what's going on? I want to see her."

"Not just yet. She is in surgery."

"Oh no! Why?"

"Miss Hall was hemorrhaging severely. I'm afraid she is having a miscarriage. The placenta detached." He pauses before elaborating. "But there is more." Jesse gazes in a complete daze. "This appears to be an ectopic pregnancy as well. I don't know how this went on undetected," he says sourly.

At Jesse's bewildered expression the doctor proceeds. That is, a baby was also growing inside of her fallopian tube. The tube ruptured and this is causing most of the pain and bleeding. We are doing all we can for her now."

Jesse is stunned into silence, but has so many questions. Annie's family come in just as the doctor is leaving. Jesse has tears in his eyes. "What's happened to my baby?" her mother shouts as she approaches him.

"She's in surgery. They say it was an ectopic pregnancy and they're trying to repair the damage." He goes on to tell them the whole story while they wait for more news.

Returning home that early evening, C.C. seemed to be troubled. When her husband came in he asked if she was ok. She nodded in a somber manner. Then she let him know the sad news that Jesse shared with her. The look on his face was shocked. He couldn't understand why she would care about this woman. This woman he had an affair.

"C.C. Why are you telling me this?"

"I thought you might want to check on her. Or at least hear about what happened. Don't you care?"

"Yes, but I didn't think you would like…"

"It really doesn't matter what I like. What's happened is extremely dangerous. You two were involved. It's the decent thing to do."

He can only stare at C.C. He thinks to himself, 'She is an amazing woman.' This was such a weird scenario: his wife suggesting he go and sees another woman.

"Go. Now!" she pushes him with tears forming. "Besides, Jesse asked for you to come."

"What! Why would he want to see me?"

"Apparently there was a reason your tests could have been negative."

Unsure as what to do, he asks again, "Are you sure?"

"Just go."

Once he's gone C.C. sits down to gather her thoughts. She was behaving so calmly at all this information, but inside she was screaming. She was happy to be there for Jesse in this trying time, but she was secretly wishing it was for something involving them. As for her husband, she refused to shed anymore tears over him and he needed to suffer any consequences for his treachery against her. She could feel her calm leaving and the anger returning. Just then, her children came downstairs laughing and jumping up into her lap. She couldn't help but smile at their adorable faces. Her daughters were so precious to her and she valued being a mother above all things. This fact alone made her sad for Annie.

Precious Child

Lull little one & close your eyes
No worries tonite
Shut your eyes and drift to sleep
I'll keep you close to my heart
You'll never be alone ~ Mama's here for you
Goodnite little one & sleep soundly
Feel my heart beat as I hold you in my arms
Always at nite keeping you safe & warm
Lullaby & goodnite to you my precious child
For when you wake, you shall see my eyes

Back at the hospital, Annie was in recovery resting very uncomfortably. The mental pain was almost as bad as the physical pains she was experiencing. She blamed herself. The doctors warned her about the risks of an amniocentesis test so early in the pregnancy and stress levels causing miscarriages. Now she may never get pregnant. Jesse sits outside the room door trying to make since of what's happened. He can hear Annie's crying from the hall. Wanting to take the pain away he had to relax his thoughts before going back in so as not to upset her further.

However, relaxing was nowhere in sight as the storm known as 'C.C.'s husband' just walked off the elevator. He finds the room, walking cautiously over to

Jesse. Jesse's face hardens at the sight of him. But he closes his eyes and takes a cleansing breath.

"Hello, I'm Dar…" Jesse cuts him off.

"I know exactly who you are. Let's not pretend here. I only asked you here because I thought you would be concerned for Annette's health." He pauses to see the reaction, and then rolls his eyes in agitation. "The doctors also informed me that the paternity tests we both took were in a way tainted due to the nature of the pregnancy. Although now that there are no more babies…"

"Babies?" he asks confused.

"Yes, babies. Apparently there were twins. Why don't you go and see Annie now. Maybe she will tell you more." Jesse walks down the hall with his head bowed. Exhaustion was overtaking his whole being.

Lost Not Found

I can't shake the notion that I've lost something so very dear.
There's an empty space somewhere, but what is it that's missing?
How can I find what I don't know is gone?
I feel a presence next to me, but nothing is there.
When I close my eyes, I see an image.
However, when they're opened it's all a blur.
There is a notion ~ Something is missing.
I'm trying to put my finger on it.

Although I'm not quite sure what I'm reaching for.
And how would I know once I had my hands on it?
Sometimes I get eerie chills,
as something familiar is just around the corner.
If I ran into it, would I recognize it?
How would I know where I lost it?
I still cannot shake the notion
that I am missing something dear.
I wish I could touch the presence I feel next to me.
I need the images I see to come into focus,
In order to find what I think I lost.

Say Yes

"Please come in and have a seat." Jesse guides C.C. to the couch in his office. "I'm sorry we had to cancel our meeting yesterday."

"Jesse, you had to deal with an emergency. I completely understand. Would you like to talk about it?"

"No. Not yet." He answers despondently. "Let's actually do a little work first. Then maybe we can talk." She could tell this has really disturbed his spirit. So she does what she does best, put him at ease.

"Ok. Let's get to work!" He smiles shyly and she strokes his cheek. Jumping up from the seat he saunters over to his desk, picks something up holding it to his chest, and then swiftly turns back.

"Surprise!" C.C.'s face lights up with glee. "You are now a published author. All you have to do is decide where you want to sell it."

She bounces out of her seat throwing her arms around his neck screaming, "Everywhere!"

Without thinking, she plants a hard, lingering kiss on his lips. They are breathless when they break away. Still panting she manages, "I can't believe it. Thank you."

"It is my pleasure. But this is all your hard work. And it's paid off. You deserve this." C.C. is ecstatic. And knowing that her dreams were finally made really blew her mind.

As work goes, they had a very productive morning. They discussed marketing strategies and future book launching. The relaxed feeling they always shared was back. As they wrapped up the day's work the two could tell they were stalling. With no other meetings for the day, Jesse offered to order some lunch.

Sitting there laughing enjoying themselves made their minds wander again. Both are having these strong feelings that cannot be denied. But both fear the response that might occur. However the events from two nights ago still hangs in the air and need to be addressed.

C.C. breaks the ice first. "How is Annie doing?"

"She's hurting," he answers solemnly. "It's going to take some time for her to heal."

"In more ways than one," C.C. whispers.

"She claims she's ok with the loss, but I know she won't be. Especially since the doctor's told her about the hysterectomy. They did all they could, but the bleeding just wouldn't stop." Jesse closes his eyes reflecting on that night. "She kept screaming 'I want my baby,' now Annie will never have children."

"How do you feel, Jesse?"

"I honestly don't know. I'm more confused than ever."

C.C. bites her lip in worry. She wants to tell him how she feels about him. But is it the right time she wonders? So she asks carefully, "Well, what will you do now?" He looks at her and C.C. is waiting patiently for him speak.

He hesitates for a moment, then replies, "I need to take care of her now." C.C. lowers her gaze. "You know, all I wanted was to be needed by Annie and now that she does, something is different. She needs me to be by her side, love and care for her while she recuperates. But things just aren't the same between us. I can't trust her anymore. I love her and wish she didn't have to endure this kind of pain, but I haven't changed my mind or my heart."

Jesse places his fingers under her chin to look into her eyes.

"What do you mean?" she cries with a quivering voice.

This intimate gesture makes her squirm in the seat.

"I will help her until she can get on her feet. I made that promise. But as I told her, I'm no longer in love with her and I will not go on hurting or denying my heart."

He holds her face in his hands. He speaks so softly to her. "Could you love me C.C.?"

Her eyes widen and her heart flutters. She all but wished he would love her and here he is asking it of her. Shock apparent on her visage.

Fear keeps her from answering directly, but then

she dares asks, "Do you want me to love you Jesse?" Tears began filling her eyes.

"Only if you love me as much as I love you." He holds her mesmerized gaze with his, not breaking contact. She nods slowly. Her answer forming:

Without A Doubt

I cannot be more ready!
I have found what I've always wanted and I couldn't be happier.
Even though I have everything,
there still feels like something is missing.
However, I cannot imagine what it is.
My most prized possessions are at hand,
what more could I need?
Any doubts I've had made me feel unsure.
So I dropped all of them when I chose the path to my future,
A future that is filled with love, support, friends & family,
Support that shelters me in times of need,
However, I still can't shake this longing feeling!
I have shredded my doubts yet
I am nervous about moving forward.
Maybe the future itself is missing in my life.
I am definitely pointing in the direction I want to take.
Of this, there is no doubt!
What has yet to come is what I'm longing for and it's missing
because it is not yet found.
My nervousness isn't fear. It's Excitement!

Excitement in taking the road less traveled
Taking on new responsibilities for someone other than myself
And sharing my life with a partner,
Rather than living selfishly alone.
I've made my decisions with an
opened mind and cleared conscience.
Free in the thought that I have absolutely NO DOUBTS.
I am secure in my reasoning.

Tears are released unbidden. "Tell me," he says forcefully. Then she answers eagerly,

"Yes I could. I love you Jesse."

Jesse captures C.C.'s mouth with his own passion dispensing all emotion within. She returns his fervor grasping his biceps. When they separate they are winded and panting. She pushes him from her to clear her thoughts for a second.

"Jesse, wait. I admit it. I do love you and think of you constantly. But I am ever hesitant," she pauses, "because I do not want this to be a rebound."

"Of course it's not C.C. My want of you is much more to be defined. I will take my time, as you should as well, in order for us to grow together." She takes his hand in hers and places it to her heart.

"I can't promise you forever. Not now. That would be unfair to both of us. But I won't pretend or ignore how deep my feelings are for you." This is what he's wanted to hear. That they both share in something stronger than pain and more comforting than sorrow.

He pulls her in his arms and she throws her arms around his neck to embrace. Here is where they promised to acknowledge their circumstances and work through them fairly and in turn allow their love for one another to be undeniable. No matter where it led them.

My Vow

At last, it is here
The day I've waited for all my life
Someone to love and cherish
And one to do the same in return
As I stand before you
It's as if looking into a mirror
We are joining as one
Same mind ~ Same heart ~ Same soul
One being
On this day, I pledge my heart to you
With my eyes wide, open
I give to you my al l~ No holding back
No barriers between us
Just opened arms allowing each other into their lives
Accepting the person, you are

Change in Status

Their love has been declared but cannot be broadcasted. So much is unresolved. The days passed but they didn't feel lonely anymore. They were happy. At least they thought they were. C.C. and her husband had to tell the children what was happening.

"So daddy can't live with us anymore?" the younger girl asks.

"He's not going right away, but soon, yes daddy is leaving." C.C. looks from the girls to him and he shakes his head in disbelief. The older girl yanks away.

"I knew you didn't love us anymore!" They all sit in horror as she continues "You're leaving us to be with that Annie woman aren't you?" she screams at her father in tears. Her mom stops her running out of the room. C.C. tries to comfort her.

"Please sit down and listen to us."

The youngest jumps in her dad's lap hugging his neck. "I love you daddy. You do love us. Don't you?"

He wraps his arms around her tightly. Softly sobbing as he does. "Of course I love you girls. And I love your mom as well. That will never change." He glances back to C.C. and she turns away. "And I'm not leaving to be with anyone else."

C.C. smirks and their daughter frowns folding her arms. She sits closer to her mom.

"Girls just listen to me. I've behaved selfishly and I've hurt you. All of you. But sometimes it's best to go away so no more damage can be done." Tears begin to run down C.C.'s face. "I'm always here for you. We're going to be ok."

"Mommy, are you ok?" The oldest girl turns her attention to her mother. She understands all that's happened in this house to her mother by the hands of her father and she doesn't like it. "Mommy I love you and I want you to be happy." She jerks her neck glaring at him then turns back to hug C.C. and whispers, "You deserve it."

Instantly she smiles and thoughts of Jesse pop into frame. Just remembering those days after their meeting was incredible. This one night their want for one another was undeniable and no one was going to take it away.

This Time It's For Real

"Jesse, would you make love to me if I asked you to?"

C.C.'s heart was racing as they lay on the floor in front of the fireplace. He placed her wine glass down and raised her chin to look at him. This was not a question he expected. This was finally their time to be together without any regrets or contemplations. Jesse wanted nothing more than to make love to C.C., but he did not want to rush her. Jesse looked into her eyes searching for any signs that she was unsure.

"Well, would you?"

He sat up and lifted her onto his lap. C.C. wrapped her legs around Jesse and he pulled her as close to him as possible. He continued to stare into her eyes. As he sweetly kissed her on the nose he exclaims, "I will do whatever you ask of me." She smiles and he says, "Let me ask you a question."

"Yes", she chirps then lightly kisses his eyes.

"Will you tell me how to love you?"

This question was surprising. C.C. had never thought to tell someone how to actually love her. She stared at him biting her lip nervously.

"I will take great pleasure in making love to you Ciara." C.C. begins to smile brighter and reach in to kiss him just as he says, "But you have to tell me what you want."

Each time that he asks her what she wants, he moves in closer to her and kisses beneath her earlobes. He can feel her shiver with every brush of his lips. The blush is now evident on her face and she is speechless.

"Tell me how you want to be loved. I want to know I'm pleasing you." Jesse's voice is so low and seductive.

C.C. had never been asked what she liked when

it came to sex. Not in any great detail. She had only ever imagined what she really wanted out of sex and let her husband set the pace. In her mind she wanted to feel electric, but didn't know how to verbally express what she wanted. Never realizing that she could. And just as she thought of the way she wished to feel Jesse spoke her thought out loud.

"When I make love to you I want you to feel desired."

C.C. wasn't used to sharing what she liked and was embarrassed to tell Jesse what she hoped he would do to her.

Jesse was sensing her apprehension so he decided to coax her a little. With feather light kisses to her neck he whispers, "How does that feel?"

C.C. moans and she can feel Jesse smile as he continues to kiss her collar bone. He grabs her derrière and she gasps as he asks, "How does that feel?"

Holding on to the sides of her face he licks her bottom lip searching for passage to mingle with her tongue. Consumed in the kiss, passion took over. He pulled her even closer to him and she could feel his erection pressing into her. She quickly pulls the shirts over their heads. As he lifted her taking to the bedroom, she held onto Jesse's neck and he lay her down on the bed making quick work of the rest of their clothing.

Jesse smoothly wraps C.C.'s leg around his waist and again asks, "How does that feel? Talk to me."

C.C. then wraps both of her legs around and pulls him into her body and answers, "It feels like I am yours."

He buries himself within her and asks, "How does it feel?"

How Does It Feel?

With that look of want and heat, you peer into me,
linking us together with a stare.
Locked in an embrace unable to separate,
I pull you closer knowing how it will feel.
As my body quivers with a simple kiss to the neck,
my loins send a signal ready to ignite
It feels so wet, as I boil to the surface.
I feel your member swell against my thigh, moist and hard
searching for the point of entry.
Tickle my doorway with the password only known to you.
Push your way forward while I guide you through my vessel:
Hot and slick ~ Mind blowing and blinding ~
In & out you slide ~ Up & down I ride.
My passageway grips you with all my might,
steering you in the direction that fits me best.
My once empty canal now filled with all of your superb
masculinity, laying the groundwork for future plowing.
Staking claim to what you now know is your property alone
Specially designed to reach maximum pleasure
Power surges running through my body

My energy level is plummeting,
but the excitement is too overwhelming to stop.
The tension cannot release!
Juices are flowing ~ Bodies perspire
Our thrusting creates convulsions making my legs lock around your waist, needing to let go with fear of erupting.
I let my vision come into focus
to gaze upon this beautiful creature.
My breathing slows finding the rhythm of your stroke.
As the tempo quickens every layer of me heats
Easy glides turning to hard pounds,
building up to a glorious climax!
Tell me you're there and I'll follow behind, landing at a destination we both have in mind.
We are coming so close to generating one soul.
This fire is intense, unable to control!
With an explosion, so infinite words cannot explain just how this moment really feels.
Don't get me wrong these are the words of how weak in the knees and toe curling I've become.
But the voice can't speak.
For occupied is my tongue, engaged in a task yet to complete.
Do not fret…I'm coming close to the end,
And you will be proud of the job I've done!
Please excuse my dazed behavior.
You are simply disrupting my nervous system.
Pleading for comfort with a sigh of relief,
I came to a light with outstretched arms and waiting to hold…
Hold this fragile frame,

declaring peace and elation putting my emotions at ease.
With my mouth regaining its moisture, the words begin to form.
Finally able to say just how it feels!

Now that he's told Annie he's not in love with her, she cries herself to sleep. He's been there for her during the recuperation but his arms seem so cold. Jesse lies next to her rubbing her back until he thinks she is asleep then goes into another room.

Annie asks him what will happen with them and he simply says, "We'll get better." Jesse kisses her forehead and walks away.

"I've lost him forever," Annie cries as she lies down whimpering. Jesse stands outside the door listening to her.

Leaning against the door he closes his eyes and sighs... "I love you Annie."

Mixed Emotions

Gone too soon
A great soul
Forever shining bright as the moon
Images of a time they were always there
Larger than life
Every move made done with flare
Now my confusion is maddening

The lights have gone dim
People keep saying it's because I'm saddened by loss
This can't be right, I still feel a presence
A presence of warmth and protection that surrounds me

As he sits trying to get through some work his mind is unfocused. He's trying to keep his promise of nursing Annie back to health, but the nagging at his heart is torture. The longer he stays here with her he prolongs the real healing for both of them.

'How can I trust her when she broke my heart?' This thought stays with him whenever he tries to comfort her. Recalling what infidelities she indulged in keeps a wall up between them. The fact makes it impossible to forgive and it's what's driving him away. That and how he yearns to be near C.C.

"Mommy you look so happy today. What's up?"

C.C. holds a copy of her book in her hands and shows it to her.

"I did it baby. I wrote a book and now I'm an author!" She jumps up and down and hugs her close.

"Wow mom! This is so cool." C.C. and her daughter are laughing and dancing about when her husband and younger daughter walk in the door.

"Hey, what's going on sissy? Are we having a party?"

"Mom has her own book!" her daughter yells.

"What! Really?" The expression on this man's face is utter surprise. It doesn't go unnoticed by C.C. or her daughter.

"Yes really dad. Look." She shoves the book at him. Staring at the cover he is stunned. But soon as he turns it to the back cover a broad smile illuminates his face.

With his youngest looking on she says, "Mommy, you look pretty!"

"She looks beautiful!" C.C.'s eyes dance with delight at his words. "I remember taking this picture. She just found out she was having you, little girl." He points to their first born child.

"Congratulations Ciara Claire," he beams.

"Thank you Darren," she responds giving him a hug.

Just then the door bell rang. The girls run to the door. There's a delivery. Two dozen long stem lavender roses are presented to C.C. Everyone's mouths gape open. Especially Darren's.

"Who is it from mommy?"

She reads the note attached and cannot stop smiling.

It reads:

'To celebrate a talented woman who also stole my heart. Congratulations C.C. You are going to be a success! Love Jesse.'

After a beat she replies, "My publisher."

At that moment, a husband and wife knew they were no more.

Look At Me Now

People said it couldn't be done
Dashing my hopes to dust
But none of that would stop me
Onward and upward, I always say

Coming from nothing and not having much
Every little bit meant so very much
I saved everything and kept it well preserved
Taking such pride, keeping its value worth

Nothing I touched would ever be worthless
Treasures created with my own little hands
Simple ideas formed out of brilliance
Pieces of scrap made into designer quality

You said that I was cheap
'Cause I didn't spend large amounts
But my words last forever
And my products weigh more than gold

Goodbye Annie

"Did you like them? I hoped you would. You said they were your favorite... You are surely most welcome."

Annie hears him on the phone as she approaches the living room.

"Well maybe if we could meet I will be the first to get a signed copy."

She can hear him laughing out loud then whispers something she can't make out. Jesse falls back against the couch and notices Annie watching him.

"C.C. I've got to go. We'll make arrangements later." He looks away for a second as he straightens up. "Good evening Ann. Do you want something?"

With sad eyes she answers, "It was so quiet. I thought I was alone. Then I heard voices."

Jesse glances down to his phone. "I hope I didn't interrupt you."

She shuffles further into the room.

"No. Come and rest here. Can I get you something?" Once settled on the couch he wraps a blanket around her.

"You should eat. I'll go get something for you."

"Were you talking to her?"

She doesn't open her eyes. He stares down at her and murmurs, "Yes I was. I didn't mean to wake you."

"Jesse, are you leaving?" She flashes her eyes at him this time.

"I was going to heat your dinner."

Trying to sit up straight Annie clarifies, "Are you leaving me?" He swallows not sure this is the time. "You can tell me Jesse. I know you're trying to help me, but I need to know so I can deal with all my pain." Jesse comes to sit beside her.

"Ann, I just need to make sure you are well enough to be here..."

"…On my own." She finishes his sentence. When he does not answer immediately, she goes on, "So you are leaving me." This was more of a statement. "Is there anything I can do to make you stay? Be with me."

"I was with you Ann. But you were everywhere but here with me." They both seem to be fighting back tears.

Trying to show she is not hurt she says, "So why don't you just go now?" Her voice betrayed the true emotions.

Jesse looks directly at Annie and answers, "Because I don't know how to let you go." Very seriously he continues. "I never planned to be without you. Now I can't stay with you in fear of my heart's confusion not to mention pain."

"Does C.C. make you happy now?"

"She makes me see."

"See what exactly?"

"See that I can be happy again. She makes me able to show my feelings openly and yes that makes me happy."

The silence that comes is deafening. Jesse silently

wills her to say something regarding his statement, but as usual she doesn't. Jesse sighs and wipes his face.

"You know we always used to have so much to say to one another. Passion was never an issue for us. Yet somewhere things seem to have slowed down and I don't know where I lost you on the way."

Annie raises her eyes to meet his and a tear is finally released.

She whispers, "Could you consider finding your way back to me? I don't want to lose you Jesse." As he wipes the droplets away he cups her face then kisses her cheek.

"Annie, I love you and I'm sorry." He pauses briefly. "But you already lost me."

Annie's body shutters and closes her eyes tightly. With his hands still on her face she reaches for his shoulders trying to pull him closer. Jesse initiates the embrace and relishes the contact as he knows in the back of his mind this is the last time he will allow it again.

The Journey Continues

"Cheers!" Jesse and C.C. clink glasses as they toast her achievements. Sitting together sharing a meal, conversation, and each other is what they've waited for. There's no one to stop what they feel and they don't hide it. This was one of the many nights they've spent together since declaring their true feelings. Each moment was cherished more than the last. But they didn't want to flaunt this budding relationship. Things were still so unfinished for them.

C.C.'s divorce wasn't finalized, but Darren had already moved out. They didn't want to confuse their children any further. He found a place of his own and they made arrangements to see the girls daily to adjust to his absence. The younger seemed to be taking it hard not living with her daddy, but the older didn't seem to care that he was gone. She's still holding resentment towards him and the treatment of her mother. She may not have known what all really happened between them, but she always hated to see her mother crying. Now that her father is not there anymore she sees nothing but smiling and laughter, especially when her mom is on the phone.

C.C. and Jesse speak on the phone every evening. When they don't see each other for work or the rare night out, just hearing one another's voice is stimulation enough. This one night their want for one another was undeniable. C.C. would never have done this or even asked for this before, but suddenly she blurted out to Jesse, "Close your eyes and imagine I'm there with you."

"Ok, now what?" he whispers.

"I'd like to try a little"….

Dirty Talkin'
{Woman} {"Man"}

Can you talk to me?

"Yes I can."

Talk dirty to me! I want to know about us. You know what I want from you. Don't try avoiding it, you know want me too.

"Whatever do you mean? What do you want from me?"

I'm not sure if you are feeling the affections I am. Whisper it in my ear. Time spent in your space, wrapped in your arms, an affectionate embrace.

"I can give you only so much. Talking dirty stimulates, but doesn't release."

It intrigues me to hear what you could do to me. Don't dwell on what can't be done, you know you want me too. I thought you liked spending time with me, even if it's to tease.

"I love it when you tease me. Gyrate your hips in front of me and ease down onto my lap. Circle around and around rubbing against me while I hold your waist in place."

Tell me how you like it. Where do you want me?

"I got you now. Look into my eyes and kiss me."

I love when I can taste you on my lips. You make me want you more.

"What do you want more of?"

Talk dirty to me!

"Say my name." "Tell me to squeeze you tighter. Say my name so I know you're only talking to me."

Do you know how much I want you? You are making me horny!

"Good, we need to do something about that."

Do what you please. Something dirty. Take me now!

"You want me to take you here?"

Yes! Take me now. You know how hot you get me don't you?

"I'm going to give you some good lovin'…in time. Hold on, it's coming."

It's so hard to resist your touch. I'm yearning some of your treats! What you do is yummy.

"I got something yummy for you!"

I know you do. What you got for me? Give it to me now. I'm so hungry! Talk dirty to me while you keep me waiting.

"Ok, kiss me."

I love your lips on me.

"Open your mouth so I can suck on that tongue."

Oh, that sounds so nice and nasty.

"Is this dirty talking' for you?"

Yeah baby, I like it nice & nasty. Deliciously salty & sweaty!

"Me too! I'm going to work up a good sweat, licking, sucking, and squeezing you to me. Feeling your thighs soaked with moisture opened wide just for me, ready for invasion, it makes my strength long and hard!"

My appetite for you is insatiable! I want you to need me as I do you.

"I want you hot for me. Crave my touch!"

I want to see you rising, growing harder and stronger.

"I have dreams of times being in your mouth."

I think I'm starting to like these dreams. I feel sexy and cannot stop thinking of you. You are my drug and I need a fix.

"I'll be your remedy, all that you need."

Jesse proclaimed, "How I wish I could be there with you. Then maybe we could play out our little fantasies." His voice is so low and filled with heat. They both give a little laugh as she inhales and says, "That will be fun!"

However, Jesse still hadn't moved out of the apartment with Annie so he tried to be considerate and not throw C.C. in her face while they still shared a home. But Jesse made it perfectly clear that their relationship was over and he was moving on. He was looking for a place of his own if she didn't want to move first.

It's a week before school is out and Annie needed to go and clear her belongings before she took her leave of absence.

"Good morning Jesse. She spies him having breakfast. Then walking further into the living room she notices there are more packed boxes than before.

"Good morning Ann. Are you going to work?"

"Yes. I have to tie up loose ends."

"Were you cleared to return?"

"I'm just cleaning out my personal effects. I'm not staying all day."

"Are you feeling up to that?"

"You don't need to worry about me." There is a harsh edge to her response.

He whispers, "But I do worry about you."

"My mom said she may help me later. Thanks for asking Jesse." She tries to soften her tone. "Will you be home tonight?"

"I can't say. I have prior engagements this evening." The smile on Jesse's face tells Annie all she needs to know.

"Are you going to be with Her?"

"Whom I choose to be with is none of your business." They stare at one another. Tension building. "I have to be going. Goodbye Ann." As he closes the door behind him he pauses with his hand on the doorknob then lets out a long sigh before walking away.

The Truth is Out

The school parking lot is in a mad rush even before the school day begins. The usual parents are dropping off students early and staff members entering the school. When Annie pulls into her space she feels a little apprehensive and hoped she wouldn't have to see anyone. But feeling like some kind of nightmare, she steps out of the car and spots the very last people she wanted to see. "This is just what I needed," she thought to herself.

"Good morning Miss Hall. How are you?" C.C. and her daughter walk up the stairs right next to Annie.

Annie closes her eyes briefly then answers, "Oh, I'm fine. Thanks for asking."

"Are you coming back to class?"

"No. I'm taking some time off."

"Well ok. Guess I'll see you around." The young girl waves to her mother and turns to go inside.

C.C. is still staring silently. Annie is looking everywhere but at C.C. She moves to walk on by and glances quickly at C.C. giving a half nod.

C.C. calls out to her. "Wait. I'd like to say something to you."

Hesitantly Annie turns back to face her. "Really? Why would you want to speak to me?"

"Well, once I say this I will never have anything more to do with you. Especially since you will no longer be my child's teacher," C.C. replies with just enough venom to make Annie gasp. "First, I just wanted to tell you how sorry I was about your loss." Annie pales and her jaw drops. "No one should have to go through that kind of pain."

"Thank you," she responds shocked and a little annoyed that she knew just what happened.

"Second, I forgive you for your part in all of this and I hope we can all move on from this ordeal."

The steam starts to rise up inside of Annie at these words. She took a step closer to C.C. with her hands on her hips. "You forgive me?" She began to laugh to herself. "You…Forgive me?"

"Yes, I do."

"You think you're innocent in all this?" C.C. stares back at her questioningly. "Poor, sweet C.C. You've got them all fooled don't you?" The anger is clear in the retort. The two women stand on the steps glaring at one another.

"I'm not fooling anyone."

"Don't give me that simple look!" C.C.'s daughter was coming back to the doorway to try and catch her mom. "You managed to charm Jesse away from me."

"Look Annie. I'm not going to argue with you

about this, because we both know that your acts of adultery pushed Jesse away from you. I suppose lying about having another man's baby was the last straw for him." C.C. was trying to keep her cool, but her own anger is barely contained.

Just as Annie opens her mouth to respond, the young girl walks up behind them. "Annie!" C.C. gasps covering her mouth and Annie turns with her eyes bulging. "You're Annie?"

"Baby Please. No!"

"This is the Annie that daddy was sneaking around with?"

"Baby, please." C.C. tries to calm her. "Not here. Come with me."

"No! This is all her fault. She is the reason you were crying all the time mommy." Her voice is getting shaky and tears are streaming down her cheeks.

Annie stands there with her eyes wide open, speechless. She's looking around noticing a small group leering at the scene. C.C. cries, "Let's go. We'll talk about this later." Her eyes begin to swell as well.

"How could you?" She can't hold her cries and shouts.

"I didn't mean for this to happen." Annie finally whispers to the girl.

But with steady determination the girl tries to continue. Then Annie almost raises her voice to halt her. "Don't do this!" C.C. is now restraining her daughter.

"Don't you dare tell me what to do! Just because

you were with my father doesn't make you my mother. I Hate You!" She turns her face into her mother's chest and cries out loudly.

Now Annie is shaking and sobbing wrapping her arms around herself. C.C. just looks into Annie's eyes and mouths, "I'm sorry", and then shakes her head. C.C. walks away with her child close to her side leaving Annie alone on the steps.

As they reach the car again C.C. turns to her daughter and wipes at her tear stained face. "It's going to be alright baby. You don't need to worry about her."

"But I heard you say she is having another man's baby." The girl is crying hysterically now.

"Shh, stop crying," she consoles. "I should not have said that out loud. I was angry. Trust me; there is nothing for you to worry about." C.C. hugs her child close again.

"But what about the baby mom? Daddy 's having another baby."

"That's enough! There is no more baby. That's all I'll say about it." When C.C. begins to drive away she tries hard not to show the pain or her tears.

The afternoon is filled with tension. C.C. tried to explain to Darren what happened at the school. He was pissed and embarrassed, but the greater feeling was hatred for him that he let this affair cause so much heartache, especially in his children. The last thing he wanted was his daughter hating him. He thought to himself, "What have I done? I've lost them all." The sadness in his heart was overwhelming.

When Jesse walks in the apartment, Annie is sitting alone in the dark living room. "Oh, you scared me. Why are you here in the dark?" He switches on the light.

"I think I've had enough of being seen." Annie's voice is barely a whisper.

After a deep sigh he asks, "What happened today?" He really didn't want to hear any complaints from her. She always made herself the victim, but he patiently waited for the reply.

With a sniffle she says, "Well first, I was accosted by your lover." Jesse started to fume, but was halted when she looked at him and continued, "But that wasn't what upset me." She gasps and whimpers. "It was when her daughter, my student, heard us and berated me for sleeping with her father and ruining her family."

Annie's heaving sobs are deafening. Jesse's look of bewilderment is staggering. "Oh my word. That is unexpected and unfortunate for both of you. I can see why that would upset you, but no child should have to be put in that position. The poor thing."

As he shakes his head and turns to close some of the boxes Annie finally looks at him. With wide eyes and an open mouth she cries, "Poor Thing! What about me? I was so embarrassed and hurt. But I was so sorry too," she whispered. "I knew her and counseled her for so long about what was angering her at home and I was the one making her pain continue." She stops to catch her breath and covers her face. Jesse simply stares at first, but then goes to comfort her. As Annie feels him reach around her shoulders she jumps.

"Annie you can't put this all on yourself. You can't control anyone else's feelings." Jesse tried to console her all while trying to keep his own feelings in check.

"But this is my punishment." She looks at him and cries harder. "My punishments were losing you and kill my only chance of having children. And to be left all alone."

Jesse holds her in his arms close to his chest. "Annie you're not being punished."

"But my babies are gone!" She screams out in pain. "And I will never be able to have any again." Her voice is strangled.

"Oh, Annie, I'm sorry this happened to you." She wraps her arms around his neck.

"Don't say that. I know you hate me, Jesse."

"Not enough to condemn you forever. I will probably always love you." He pauses and whispers, "That's what hurts the most. But I do not hate you."

She squeezes his neck tighter and he pulls her into his lap. After a few quiet moments Annie lifts her head and asks, "This is goodbye isn't it?"

"Yes it is Annette." But he doesn't let her go. He stands with her in his arms, looks into her eyes and says, "Let me take you to bed. You're exhausted." Jesse carries her to the bedroom and gently lays her down. Surprisingly he does not leave her. Instead he wraps himself around her until she falls asleep. As they lie in silence Annie speaks.

"Jesse?"

"Yes."

"Thank you for always loving me."

He kisses her hair and soon they are fast asleep. The next morning Jesse will have left the apartment for good.

A New Chapter

"Mommy, are you happy daddy's gone?" C.C.'s youngest daughter asks sadly.

Her smile slips slightly as she answers, "No. Why would you say that?"

"You are always laughing on the phone and smiling when you go out."

"Aww, sweetheart I miss your daddy too sometimes. But I am very happy these days. Today is a special day for me too baby."

"Is that why we're getting all dressed up?"

"Yes. My book is being launched to the public." Hesitantly she continues. "And there's someone I'd like you to meet."

The older girl chimes in. "Is it who you're always talking to? They make mommy smile," she announces to her little sister. She and C.C. have a big grin on their faces.

"Yes he is my publisher. But he is also very special to me."

"He!" They are both shocked, but for different reasons. "Mommy, you met somebody else, already?"

"I've known him for some time. We've grown quite close."

"Well I think that's great mom. He just better make you happy." C.C. giggles and kisses her forehead.

Walking into the hall C.C. is overwhelmed. There are so many people looking at the new publications. Tables and booths are set up to display various authors and vendors. Photographers and members of the press are taking aim with cameras and video cameras waiting to ask questions and take pictures.

"This is so exciting!" C.C. exclaims.

"Mommy is this all for you?"

"Ha ha ha. No baby. Not all of it. But a little piece, yes." C.C. begins to tear up as she suddenly spots her name and a poster size image of her book. They walk hand in hand to her table.

"There's so many books mommy."

"Not for long." Jesse says from behind them. "People are looking to buy already."

C.C. turns to see him and smiles brightly. "Hello Jesse. I'm so happy to see you."

He reaches out to take her hand kissing it gently. When he spies the girls beside her he beams. "Who do we have here?"

"I'd like you to meet my daughters. Girls, this is Jesse. The man I was telling you about." The girls smile and say hello politely.

"Well hello young ladies. I've heard so much about you." The youngest girl moves closer to her mother, but the older pipes up and reaches for his hand to shake.

"Nice to meet you Jesse. I've heard things about you," she says and glances at her mother. "My name is Laura and this is my sister Violet. She's just shy."

C.C. smiles lovingly at her and turns back to Jesse. "Alright then, we've got work to do. Where do we start?" Jesse laughs.

He walks over to her table to set her up next to the books and very soon a small crowd has grown around her display. The video cameras join to interview C.C. about the premise of her book and when to expect a book signing.

"This is so exciting!" She is overjoyed.

Jesse brushes his fingers down her cheek and says, "It's only going to get better."

Just then a few young ladies come over to pick up a copy of the book. One woman blurts out, "This is beautiful. You've got to read this." Another continues, "This is hot! Check this out." She begins to read aloud from

'How Does It Feel?'...

'I feel your member swell against my thigh, moist and hard
searching for the point of entry.
Tickle my doorway with the password only known to you.
Push your way forward while I guide you through my vessel:
Hot and slick ~ Mind blowing and blinding ~
In & out you slide ~ Up & down I ride.'

C.C. and Jesse both gaze at each other shyly knowing the inspiration for that entry. "Wow! It's like they read my mind. Listen to this from

'Craving'...

'I crave for the burning sensation
Know that you are my extinguisher
Pressure points responding to only your touch
Bringing my body under your submission'

She giggles. "Who's the author?"

"She's right here," Jesse announces proudly. "Allow me to introduce you to this fabulous writer."

C.C. blushes as he caresses her shoulder. The ladies notice the passing look between them and ask, "Are we able to purchase the book?"

"Absolutely!" Jesse answers. "On one condition..." C.C. looks nervously at him. "You tell everyone you know how great a read it is." Everyone begins to laugh.

"Can we get an autograph?"

"Wow, an autograph! Mommy, you're famous." C.C. hugs her baby with tears in her eyes.

"It would be my pleasure."

As she signs the young women's copies and answers their questions, Jesse shocks C.C. by saying, "She will be reading at and official signing later this week."

With a look of surprise and gratefulness on C.C's face she pops out of the chair and throws her arms around Jesse's neck. "I can't believe this is all happening," she cries.

"Well believe it. Everyone will love you." C.C. kisses his cheek as he whispers, "But not as much as I do."

"Thank you Jesse, for everything. I love you too."

Just the Beginning

The week flew by and it was the afternoon of C.C.'s book reading. It was symbolic for her and Jesse because the event was being held at the local coffee house where they met. They often had poetry readings here, but this Saturday people would be coming to hear C.C.

C.C. was once again shocked to see a banner with her name on it for the world to see. The shop owner welcomes her with open arms. Taken by surprise she responds, "I didn't think you knew who I was."

"Of course I do. It's my job to know who sits in my shop and types away sipping at cold coffee." He gives C.C. a wink. "Why do you think I agreed to allow your friend here to set this all up?"

Just then Jesse walks over to them smiling broadly. "And I thought it was because you recognized a shining star." Jesse wraps his arms around C.C. pressing her close to him. When he pulls back he stares into her eyes then bends to brush his lips lightly against hers.

As they break away panting C.C. exclaims, "I don't know if I'm ready for this."

Jesse holds her gaze and reassures, "You're going to be great! I'll be right here with you."

The crowd swells quickly in the shop. All are anxious to hear from this new poet. As C.C. readies to begin she introduces herself and gives a little background of the selections chosen to present to the audience. Just then she sees her daughters walk in with her ex-husband and she pauses. Apprehensively she goes on, nervous to speak in front of Darren. Then she spots her daughter Laura giving her thumbs up. C.C. smiles and gives a small wave to her. She proceeds to read…

When the Muse Strikes

When your muse strikes, it's a wonderful feeling!
To have a light go off inside of you and brighten up the darkness surrounding your mind,
As you put pen to paper each phrase flows like an endless stream. The words are delivered directly to your brain knowing exactly what to say.
Catchy & insightful ~ Deep & passionate
Everything ever wondered becomes clear and is able to express every thought within with just a stroke of the hand. An open and non-judgmental outlet of free expression
to be poured into life.
The muse knocks the senses about leaving guided paths and directions to each allowing them to be awakened. These senses

experience fresh, new revelations
that suddenly heighten in all things.
Smells are divine
Tastes are delectable
Touches are sensitized
Hearing acute to all that's around
Visions are extraordinary
Feelings of renewed existence restored by given the written word profound descriptions to its features. These words bring reasoning to any doubts and clarity to misunderstanding.
Every endeavor now has purpose and meaning for its creation.
Lyrically orchestrated as the pen glides without hesitation.
An unspoken verbal depiction carefully designed by its author.
The muse strokes the creator's essence causing motivated inspiration in the production of the written word.

Just as she ends the first poem the room claps in appreciation and Laura turns to her dad and says, "Mom looks great up there. Everyone really likes her."

He looks to take it all in. He spots Jesse standing off to the side beaming at C.C. "Yes I see they do," he responds through gritted teeth.

"Thank you. Thank you so much. If you'll allow me I have one more I'd like to share with you. It's called…

He Makes Me Smile

The realization that I have what everyone else wants is boastful.
So many tell me how lucky I am to possess such a find and it makes me appreciate my gift.
The gift of happiness!
Who would have thought my joy could be envied?
I guess I can't blame them.
I've got the best thing in the world,
Someone to share my world!
To share everything!
My heart
My time
My thoughts
The loneliness experienced evaporated as my skies cleared.
Laughter so thunderous the resounding wails
washed away my tears.
An entity with such presence the mere sight gives off a warm sensation throughout my being.
My soul comes alive knowing I am wanted by my gift from above… Loved by my special gift!
I know love in my life!
Just before she reads the last two lines,
C.C. turns toward Jesse and finishes…
I have so much love, respect,
and understanding through this find.
I never thought I would surrender myself
to this heavenly creature.

Jesse winks at her knowingly. And because he never took his eyes off of him, Darren notices the gestures passed between them frowning and narrowing his glare. Laura saw the blushing smile on her mom's face as well and knew she must be thinking of someone special.

"Oh look! There's Jesse."

"What!"

"There's Jesse. He's mom's special friend."

"How do you know him?" he says with an edge in his tone.

"We met a few days ago." Then she whispers, "I think he loves her." She giggles.

Darren looks at her gaping, but says nothing. The clapping of the crowd gets everyone's attention again and they hear C.C. ask, "Does anyone have any questions for me? Please feel free."

Several questions are asked and C.C. responds feeling at ease in this setting. Until someone fires at her, "What other changes have you made since writing this book?"

She looks around to see who asked the question and sees Darren stand staring at her. She takes a deep breath before answering and replies directly to him. "I've learned to express all of my feelings and not bottle things up. I'm…

Finding My Way

There was a time in my life
when I felt lost with nowhere to turn.
I was in a funk and could not understand why?
Why was everything so boring?
Nothing was ever satisfying.
Depression came upon me, but why?
I loved life and needed to embrace it.
There was nowhere to turn.
I had no outlet ~ I had to get out.
Everything trapped inside and no one knew what was wrong.
But then I opened my mouth to sigh and complain ~
Instead, notes & words came out.
The words just flowed ~
Harmony was restored ~
Now I was no longer silenced.
I was being muffled and did not have the words.
What once was hidden, buried within,
is now released for all to hear.

"This is the beginning of the journey back to me." He sits back down breaking their eye contact. She takes a sip of water then speaks to the crowd. "I want to thank you all for taking the time to come out today. I also want to leave you with…

A lil piece of me

I love sharing a lil piece of me! My thoughts and views or cares and concerns…it's therapy for me. I write to let off steam usually, it helps to talk through the pen or pencil, and not always to a person…they don't always understand (no matter how hard they try). I love to share a lil piece of me, even though everyone doesn't understand the pieces. Frustration and anxiety is released and a cleansing breath is allowed and greatly welcome. I hope you understand this lil piece of me and thank you for the chance to share it with you and maybe you will share a lil piece of you with me!

'Til we meet again.

The crowd stands and applauds and C.C. moves through the room to shake hands. Jesse walks over to her with his copy of the book in his hand. "Hello. May I have your autograph?"

She has a huge grin on her face and says, "But of course! Anything for a fan." They both laugh. "Who should I make it out to?"

He recites, "To Jesse, the love of your life."

C.C. glances up through her lashes and blushes. Then she reads aloud her writing…

With all my love to share with you.
Always,
The love of your life.

C.C. closes the book, raises her head to look at Jesse and gives him a wink.

Epilogue

One year later…

C.C. stops in front of a book store that carries her book. As they walk inside Jesse picks up a copy and holds it out to her.

"Well here I am a real live author. I can't believe so many people actually wanted to read the thoughts in my mind."

"Well believe it C.C. I told you that your words would be heard. The sales from the book proved that and now the printers have them on back order because so many people ordered your book." Jesse was so proud of the woman standing beside him.

"It's still so hard to believe how far I've come since I began writing this." C.C. ran her fingers across the front cover with tears in her eyes. "It's just as I imagined."

As she returned the book to its place on the shelf she stated, "I've finally learned how to express all of my feelings and not bottle things up and I've been able to express it through my writing. This is truly the beginning of the journey back to me. I cannot believe I've already finished the first half of the new book."

Jesse turns her to look at him. "Love is also a journey and it makes decisions from the heart. Now will you consider taking the journey with me as my wife?"

Jesse has asked C.C. to marry him numerous times and each time she has said no or it's not the right time. She started remembering the first time he proposed to her...

He Planned the Perfect Evening

He loves me and wants to please me!
He wants to take me away.
He wants only to be We.
He called to tell me his need for me.
Missing my scent and the feel of my body,
he whispers in my ear to tell me his plan.
Looking in my eyes with a smile on his face, he says, "
I'm pretty" and I melt.
We both quiver when I lean in to kiss his neck.
Oh, how I love you!
Kissing my lips as the sun sets around us
with the warm breeze over our skin.
He undresses me slowly as my bath is drawn.
Heavenly aromas secrete the air.
Spectacular views inspire the mind and my giggle
& smile are more amazing to his senses.

I'm bathed with the utmost care, dried lightly,
and then laid down surprisingly.
He readies me for the hot oil rub, gliding his palms ever so
gently but firmly across my cooling flesh.
Decadent treats of wine and sweets fed to me
as offerings all for my pleasure.
He plans to please me perfectly!
With no expectations and no interruptions,
there is only We.
Private access in an unchartered region
Private dining with the most exotic meals
Perfect plans of unlimited desires!
This man, who adores me alone, waits on me without
hesitation, planning an evening of perfect stimulation.
I'm cherishing every moment he plans for the evening.
He makes me smile and he makes me glow.
Such pleasures arise during his plans for me!

It was perfectly beautiful and she wanted nothing more than to say yes. Her daughters had grown fond of Jesse and since the divorce; they were able to be closer than ever. Everything in her heart wanted to say yes to Jesse's proposal, but she just wasn't ready to.

Over the year it is Jesse who has stood by her side while she went through the divorce and the success of her book. He loved her more and more every day and he knew she loved him too. However, she had finally found a path that was hers alone to follow. Although she gained so much joy and pleasure from the new love she found with Jesse, she didn't know when or if she ever wanted to marry again. Not yet, at least.

C.C. cried, "Jesse you know how much I love you. I'm just not ready," She caressed his face and placed her hand over his heart.

He closed his eyes and grabbed her hand. Then pulling her closer to his frame he gives her a soft kiss of the lips and replies, "I love you too and I won't stop asking you to become my wife."

C.C. wraps her arms around his neck and answers, "I don't ever want you to."

They left the store walking arm in arm content in what the two of them shared.

Jesse pulled out his copy of her book. "Read it to me. I never tire of your words."

C.C. smiled as she took it from his hands and began to read to him saying…

"Inspire & Motivate"
Poetry for the Heart & Mind
By…Me!

She giggles to herself at this accomplishment and continues to read all of the poems that expressed all of her inner most thoughts.

Inspire & Motivate

Inspiration comes from the life lessons
we view in our everyday life.
Everyone has the ability to be an inspiration!
Motivation is the drive to be more than ordinary.
Motivate your dreams to become reality!
If your dreams are never realized,
They will only exist as fantasy!

What Do I Do?

What do I do for you?
I know I would do anything for you
I give all of my love to only you
But tell me, what do I do for you?

I'm keeping my heart open
Open for your every desire
How do I know it's enough?
Tell me, what I do for you

I've never questioned how far I would go for you
But without a word that lets me know where I stand,
Shows me I am doing all that I can,
How do I know what I do for you?

So tell me what do I do for you?

Reassure my heart that I am all you need…
That nothing can compare to the love we share…
Our souls have met and rested within
All these things you do for me

Tell me my love…what do I do for you?

On Your Wedding Day

You have come together to be united.
Together you've created your own family
that can't ever be divided.
As you stand before God pledging your love to one another,
Know that everyone you love- here and in spirit- is behind you.
Guiding and supporting you on your journey to time indefinite.
What once was 'yours and mine' is now 'Ours'.
So keep sharing and loving one another, that is the key!
With faith, trust, commitment and devotion in your hearts,
A happy life you will live.

Pledge

With you, I have no fear.
You are the reason why.
Why I rise with the sun awaiting your smile
With a beating heart anxious to hold you near.
You've shown me what it means to be truly loved.
I give you my heart filled with an abundance of love, faith
And the acceptance of yours in return.
You've opened my eyes to what I thought was a dream,
But I see that it is real life.
My life that today I share with you.

Best Friends

B Beautiful
E Eager
S Strong
T Thoughtful

F Faithful
R Respectful
I Intelligent
E Equal
N Natural
D Devoted
S Survivors

Wife, Mother, and Teacher

I got everything I always wanted
Typical all American family
And the job of a lifetime
Who could ask for more?
Do I deserve to ask for more?
If I do, what else could I ask?
More than my husband, kids, and home
I could enjoy my days and love what I did
What's better than that?
Who could ask for more?
Do I deserve to ask for more?

I thought I had it all
Freedom, time, and togetherness
But when I open my eyes
I'm all alone
I don't have to work ~ No one to answer to
But my job never ends ~ I feel like a slave
I thought I was the queen of the castle
But I fell I'm being over thrown
Where is my knight in shining armor?
Too busy slaying dragons
Is this what, ever after looks like?
Will I ride off into the sunset?
Now it's too late
Labor Day is here and my summer is over

Always By My Side
[To my B.F.F]

All my life I've had someone to turn to.
Someone who would never judge me,
From the time I was a small child.
In grammar school, my best friends equaled two.
One I looked like & the other shared a birthday.
In Junior High, my best friend can just in time.
We were homesick and from the same place.
We've always had so much in common.
In High School, my best friend was destined to be.
They came out of nowhere, but led me to my future.
A future with my eternal best friend.
We have had many firsts together.
We came from the same place as well.
This best friend is my destiny.
We have a bond sealing our lives forever.
I've had someone by my side in every point of my life.
Each one essential to who I am,
Making me be more open to love and life.
Each one will always be by my side.

Willing to Share

What makes a friend
Is it being close when the world seems so far away
Is it understanding, when everything else is confusing
Finding friends is always an easy task
But keeping them is where the true test comes to play
Some find they have friends to turn to
But how many actually can count on you
How can you be sure you are a true friend
True friendship is without limitations
No restrictions hold you back from being yourself
A real friend builds you up
Never tearing you down
Good friends never lie to you
But will keep your secrets
What makes a friend
Friends are made when you have love in your heart,
Peace of mind,
And faith in your soul

Let You In

There was no fear in my heart or a doubt in my mind
That you would be let in, no questions asked
I didn't stop to think ~ I went with my gut
No pondering the precautions
Only going on pure desire
Love at 1st. sight ~ who thought it existed
My eyes welcomed you in playing hostess to my heart
However, I knew I was letting in danger
Danger yet assurance
The danger of opening up completely
Opening up to let love in
No matter the duration and the assurance
that my heart does not lie
Believing and trusting my heart won't let me down
My arms greeted you ~ giving you passage
A free ride without expectations or destination of the trip
No limitations on how far I'd let you go
My body entertained the thought of you
Thoughts of wanting and needing you flowed through my veins
Wanting you to let me into YOU
Needing to be excepted and desired as I do you
Vastly approaching the gateway to my heart
I wave you on still fearless ~ without doubt
But with wholehearted anticipation for what is in store

As I let you into my heart ~ you graciously enter in silence
Tiptoeing as not to bruise me with your 1st. step
Although the prints leave a defining mark
Letting you in is all I could do to get close to you
So in you came ~leaving me with memories and feelings that could never be wiped away
Good or bad, I let you in
I let you in each chamber of my heart
Where I allowed you to play ~ with no rules
Until I could take no more games
For the games you played were more than two players and I already knew so many of those
I thought I would play doubles, but ended up playing alone
By letting you in ~ my heart started to tighten
Trying to expel what I couldn't tell was bad for me
Facing my pain would force me to let you out
When all I ever wanted was to let you in

Just an Illusion

Things are never what they appear to be.
Beautiful to the eyes, but repulsive under the surface
And what seemed to be calming, made you pull your hair out.
Just an illusion playing tricks on you.

You think you read people like a book,
But as you turn their pages, the words become unclear.
Proving they are masterminds at their own game
Turning the tables and you no longer know the rules.
All these illusions pulling the wool over your eyes.

Expressions from a distance are never expressed in person.
Ashamed of the truth only unearths falsehoods
Denying what your heart needs
Just to settle on what is easily accessible.
Illusions of the heart
Casting shadows over the soul.

Crime & Punishment

Guilty as charged?
Punished for crimes I never committed.
With my peers as the jury,
I stand before them ~ Unsure of what I have done.
Maybe I am guilty by association.
Is it the company I keep or is it the lifestyle I chose?
I was unjustly tried and questioned.
My side was never heard and my words perceived as lies.
What could I do to end this execution?
The book is being thrown at me
and I still don't know my crimes.
I'm being punished with a profile that doesn't fit my description.
How can I clear my name?
But why do I have to defend myself?
My sentence is upon me and I have no course of action.
Am I guilty as charged?
Will my peers see I've committed no crime?
As I stand here before you ~ with the verdict now in,
I wait for the judge to tell me if I am guilty as sin.

Want What I Want

What I want in my heart isn't what's good for me
My heart wants more than I deserve
I can be selfish
If I deny my desires, am I betraying my heart?
My heart has many chambers
All of which long to be filled
I tend to indulge
My mouth craves the waters that flow far from my reach
The strength of my heart urges me to test the waters
Knowing this place is forbidden

Denial

I could never be mad at you
After all, you did to hurt me
I never placed the blame
In my eyes, you could do no wrong
However, deep down inside I know you were at fault
At fault for all my tears
At fault for all my heartache
I could never speak of the crime you committed
Because I didn't want it to be true
My love could never be so cruel
My love would never –
Then why are you gone
Why am I crying over you
Why am I in such denial

Worthy Praise

Does giving praise boost you up?
Is it always worth giving?
I value your praise.
It makes me feel good.
But I was only doing my job.
Does the praising make me conceded?
How much does it take to get a swelled head?
Just because I don't stand out,
does not mean I need to shout about.
My self-esteem is very high.
How often do I deserve your praise?
Why am I being singled out?
Don't worry, I don't feel ignored.
I know my worth!

Don't Count Me Out

I know you think I'm bad,
But I'm looking for some attention!
You put me down when I don't meet your standards,
So I don't even make an attempt.
I act out 'cause you don't recognize me
You don't recognize me 'cause I don't act the way you do.
I don't have what you have,
Don't see what you see,
We live very different lives.
Don't count me out!
You wouldn't learn or remember my name if I walked by,
So I get in your face.
Now you can't stop calling my name!
You'll never forget who I am!
You cannot count me out!

Inspirational Design

Through life I have seen &
learned what inspiration looks like -
And it is Beautiful!
When I see Inspiration, I see fire –
And it Burns!
Burns images into me that can never be extinguished
Images of holding hands or wiping t
he brow when you're feeling down
Images of knowing what comes next without a word mentioned
I see the beauty of inspiration in the softness of the voice that calls your name
Or in the eyes that seem to dance &
smile when you gaze with longing
These visions have engraved a since of understanding & appreciation for the little things that mean so much
I have learned that Inspiration is dedicated -
Dedicated to being true to self when
others try to bring you down
And dedicated to finding & keeping
a love that allows you to do so
Inspiration is committed –
Committed to faith & caring that leads to an eternal love with much work involved
I have seen Inspiration and it is compassionate –

Compassionate & Endless
Endless in that it continually grows with
expansion of life and grows in strength
A strength that holds firm in determination
of love & happiness
With this view of Inspiration my heart has created
a drive & the motivation to make love endure!

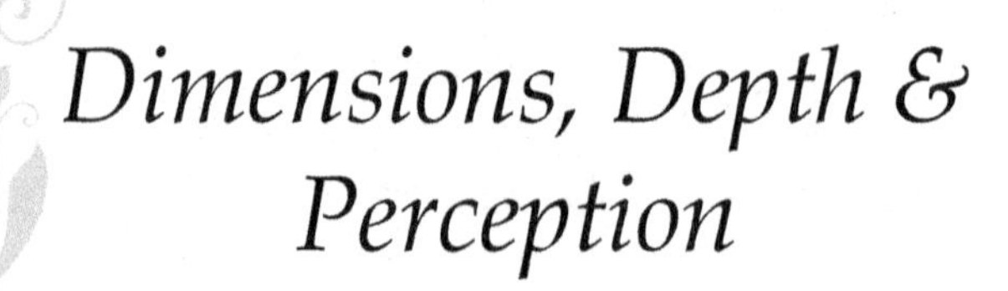

Dimensions, Depth & Perception

The dimensions of a physical being appear to be touchable,
though more often they keep themselves beyond arms length, out
of sight and with great distance
between the worlds around them.
Much like their hearts that are empty, empty because they don't
know the true depths of themselves,
how far they are able to thrive.
The perception of oneself is only what you allow or dream it to
be and thoughts of impossibility and inadequacy
hinders all ability to achieve.
With a mindset of fear or insecurity and unworthiness,
you can never reach unimaginable heights.
Heights of love & union
Heights of consciousness & understanding
Heights of respect & responsibility
A concept of perception in life reaches a greater depth
than that of the dimensions lay before them.

Barriers

The want I have cannot be denied.
The obstacles lying before me show no faltering.
What do you do when the desire is stronger
than the consequence?
The goals set bring me pleasure,
But when the road to travel leaves you unsure, it makes the
temptation so easy to veer off course.
When sentimental memories are put against intense moments,
which one wins?
The doors to a heart swing both ways.
The problem is what you find on either side.
A Barrier!
A barrier to keep me safe from harm, safe within routines,
safe in the thought that I need protection.
A barrier to keep me from my dreams,
keep me from spontaneous actions,
keep me from wanting more than what I already know.
My want cannot be denied though the obstacles may seem rough.
My mind is telling me to go easy, take it slow.
My heart is pulling me away, away to the craving that aches
inside of me.

Patience

Patience & Time
Is what I need to feel at ease and get positive results,
for which I plead,
But time waits for no one
And my patience is wearing thin.
I want satisfaction now!
The longer I wait the greater my needs.
Patience is what I need,
Time to take it slow and enjoy present emotions.
My temper is rising and I just need to breathe,
But each breath is shallower than the last.
My rage is out of control!
As I close my eyes, patience is what I call on.
Calling on "Patience" to sooth my internal beast,
Time lapses and the roaring sensation are still climbing.
"Patience!" I scream inside my head.
Patience & Time
Is all I need, it will come.
Patience!
Give it time ~ Time to come at its leisurely pace.
Patience!
It's coming…to quiet the storm engulfing within me.
With patience and time,
just when I can take no more of this angry inferno,
An eruption so painfully calm flows over and through me
Patiently & in its own time.

I Want To Know

If I knew what you wanted
I could give it to you
Tell me what I don't know
Your face I read, but with unsure definition
Tell me what you want from me
I'm here for the asking
I need to know what you need
I only have an idea
Tell me
Tell me what I must do
What must I do to tell the signs
Understand the signs that show me how to please you

Desire In Question

What would you do to have your heart's desire?
To what lengths would you go to achieve it?
If obstacles were blocking your endeavor to obtain these desires,
Would they be stronger than your will to possess it?
What is your heart's desire?
Your heart's desire is the greatest of your needs!
Your head knows what it should want.
Your body knows what it feels it wants.
But what does your heart want?
Do you know what is truly wanted in your heart?

Craving

Craving what I need
Nourishment for the soul
It's not food I need to feed
You alone possess what will fill
I crave for the burning sensation
Know that you are my extinguisher
Pressure points responding to only your touch
Bringing my body under your submission
This craving is like a drug (Addictive)
But sustains me from day to day (Naturally)
Pulsing through my veins
Running its course back & forth through my heart
My cravings for what you offer are:
Powerfully weakening ~ Momentarily fleeting
But at the same time
Dangerously securing ~ Blissfully eternal
This craving that I need makes me weary
Although once I sink my teeth in, I become lightheaded still
While my hunger can be eased by the sustenance, you provide
My craving is intensified with each delectable bite
Ooh, this craving!
I long for the taste
Tasting oh so sweet – Sweet as wine
Feeling oh so smooth – Smooth as silk
Craving what I need
I fear I will never get enough
My appetite rapidly increasing
Hungry for yet another morsel

Will You Let Me

Taste the sweetness of your lips
Suckle to my heart's content
Breathe in the fragrance you secrete
Handle your frame with comfort & care
Caress the parts that tickle my fancy
Cradle your head against my heaving bosom
Lay beside you to bask in the beauty of you
Keep you always
Revel in amazement the pleasure I have found
Share my secrets only you could understand
Take my fill of you 'til the hunger subsides
Partake in the warmth from your strong embrace
Drown in the pooling flow of your essence
Become joined with your being
Will you let me

State of Being

Up the river without a paddle
Flying blind
Lost in the sauce
Confusion @ its best
Helplessness without refuse
A state of mind I frequently visit
Two nickels to rub
Pot to piss in
Poverty @ its worse
Destitution without security
The state of living that I cannot seem to change
Round & round dizzier as I go
Spinning like a top and my mind will not focus
Scrimping and saving never getting ahead
Just barely keeping my head above water
Out of control situations that arise, have me free falling
Falling fast, falling faster, falling down
I just cannot get up
I am helpless in the world I live in
Surrounded by uncertainty, unable to find good fortune
Awake in a nightmare reeling with doubt &
second-guessing for my safety
Where can I turn for the solace and security of my future
Is there understanding of my circumstances or simply

consequences of my actions
Am I to blame for the conditions in which I exist
I just wonder if all I do is exist
Because in this life I live, I don't live my life
It's determined by my wealth and status in society
My worth is over-shadowed and lost at times, often lost to myself, creating misunderstood concepts of worthlessness
I'm clawing at my flesh uncomfortable in my own skin
While climbing the walls that close in on me
Scared there's no way out of my present state

Only I Can Hear It

Coming to grips that life is not perfect,
I've made peace with my imperfections.
I'm not the only one losing my mind.
There are voices in my head,
but it's not always such a bad thing.
The voices ask me questions. I may answer back.
But I'm not losing my mind.
I just need to weigh my options within myself.
I know I'm not perfect and often I need help.
So, I talk to myself. Who knows me better than me?
I need advice and I need therapy, but I'd rather listen to myself
than someone else putting their two cent in what I need.
So I talk to myself ~ I know I'm not perfect.

Not Afraid

To all of those who feel offended by my words,
You Should!
Because I'm not afraid to let my voice be heard above all.
I'm not the one that never speaks their own mind- following the rest of the herd.
I am here stirring up the crowd, not nodding in agreement with what was already said aloud.
If my words offend you and you take them to heart,
It's only MY truth (worldviews).
Learn to let things roll off your back.
What doesn't pertain to you set that world apart.
I'm not afraid to make people mad.
I expect a challenge, a talent most lack-
Lack in skill or know how,
Not just the ability to succeed.
However, if you're afraid to get mad,
you are not worth this race.
I brag and I boast about the things I've done & have because I've earned them.
You may disagree, but I'll never know.
You're afraid to say so.
Don't sit on the side having others speak for you.
Get out and don't be afraid to move out of the place you call safe,

Because I am not afraid!
I can go, do, be, and say whatever comes to mind without hesitation or correction from those whom you are afraid.
Fear of life & its creation
Fear of success & its ability to achieve it
Fear of growth & its need to be nourished
Fear of existing in a world we must ALL interact.

Gift

Life as a whole can't be compared
Yet so many people don't value its worth
Those who can create it- Take it for granted
Life is cheapened and made light of
Made to be a burden or chore
Life should be reviled and honored
Made to be precious or priceless
To make life take a backseat to what others
deem important is selfish
One life doesn't make the world go 'round

My Life

My life as a child wasn't my life to live
I knew things a child should never have known
Learned phrases and did not know the meanings
Knew actions without knowing how to perform them
I gained so much knowledge in such a little time
I knew I would get older, but not how fast I would grow

Trying Not to Complain

I'm not quite where I want to be. A course was set, plans made, but the destination is still out of reach.
The struggle is real! But no one really knows.
I work through it and keep on pushing,
all while hiding my predicament.
The smile on my face is simply painted on.
For the searing pain is too much to bear.
I mean, who wants to see me crying?
Bottled up and ready to pop…
I'm screaming inside for my prayers to be answered, but it seems like I am all alone.
This life is passing me by, not being lived at all.
Just going through the motions, every day repeats the next with no change in scenery.
Seasons may change,
Years have come and gone,
Although here I sit~ stuck!
Standing still – No enhancement in sight.
This is just not where I wanted to be.
There are things that are missing.
Or maybe they're merely not filled yet.
Just feeling out of place and uncomfortable in my own skin.
I've got to remap my course.
So used to traveling and running,

flying by the seat of my pants,
Where did I get off course?
Got to get off this merry-go-round!
There's no thrill in spinning in slow circles.

Fragile

**Disappointment*
**Let down*
**Broken promises*

When you wear your heart on your sleeve,
disappointment and heartache are inevitable
You put yourself out on a limb and with every broken promise
you snap from the weight it bears
Lies & deceit etched in your mind causing trust to disappear
That feeling of being let down once being
built up time after time
Nothing left but a stabbing gash that widens
with each promise broken
So scared to let others in, you keep a shield around yourself
blocking out all of the frequent disappointments
Broken promises are now shattered dreams
Your rays of hope consumed by the shadows of doubt
The heart is open to anticipation and elation of the possibilities
But it's wide open to the coy disguises that are hiding within,
never to know what's true or false

Persuasion of the Mind

Waiting till the time is right
I sit and feel that too much time has passed to go on.
How can we go on living a lie?
Being so unhappy and unsatisfied, is it anyone's fault?
Can't give up on the idea though
Persuasion
Waiting 'til the time is right is worth the wait.
Without turning away from any opportunity
Instead seizing the moments that make you
ponder the risks involved
Persuasion to keep you moving forward
Never hesitating in decisions that change the course ahead

Selfish
(A Child's Starvation)

Thinking of only yourself, ignoring the needs of others
A little of your time is all that's asked,
but you have better things to do
Little lives are being denied and priorities neglected
The exposure that is required to gain understanding is thought
to be a waste of time
Annoying and aggravating are the words uttered
Comprehending the importance of your presence goes unnoticed
While you concern yourself with frivolous and material goods
There's an endless hunger burning inside that cannot be filled
Nourishment
Substance
Availability of self is a must
Consequences for your actions will be answered
The lack-luster attitude for someone other
than yourself will be your undoing
Because your day to be cared for is coming
Selfishness will surface once more,
but this time no one will be thinking of you

Display of Love

I pledge my life to you
A man that knows how to love a woman
A woman that makes every day brand-new
Your love makes life worth living to the fullest
With you, I've found that love is real
Not an illusion to hide behind
You made it possible to be loved by my love
I've given up a life all alone
And created a union with someone forever to hold
We've been blessed with the greatest gift know
Unconditional love
Wholehearted love
Everlasting love
On this day we are joined as one

Out of My Head

Get out of my head!
I keep screaming inside to keep the thought
from streaming through my mind.
Musical lyrics belting out every emotional phrase
that stirs up memories of you.
Playing out repeatedly, over and over in perfect sync
with my beating heart.
This heart that has embedded roots within, so deep,
weeding is futile.
Fantasized images in vivid color,
So blinding with power as a beacon
that continues to draw me near.
What can I do to get away? Stay away?
Stay away from this love that is filled with pain.
Not a physical pain, but a mental state
that leaves an aching throb.
Get out of my head!
My mind doesn't want you leaving a trace,
Nevertheless, this heart pounds ever stronger.
Creating burning tears at the thought of releasing you.
How do I release a peg that fits securely in place?
Anger! Yes, anger weakens the hold.
This strangling hold you have over me that cut off my airways.
Yet blows life into me with such force I can't find my bearings

and the ager subsides once more.
But yes, I do feel anger
Moreover, its evidence is present when I consider the reasons
why you are rooted in my heart and not by my side.
I need you out of my head!
Clearing away the cloud of confusion,
Then maybe I can focus on the true anguish at hand.
Why is my anguish so conflicting?
I'm having trouble finding the strength to let go and pull away.
Something so great could not have been a mistake.
To simply say, goodbye forever…
This is where the struggle is persistent
I want you to get out of my head!

Writer's Block

Mind racing
So many thoughts
But too much information, the ideas won't form
Plans in motion
Preoccupied by all the commotion
Distracted by determination
Determined to avoid distractions
Voices growing louder
Visions going blurry
The space in my head crowded with images
and words turning to gibberish
I knew what to say to get through the task
Ugg- my mind is racing with so many thoughts
There's too much information colliding with each new idea
Sounds are becoming trapped in my head
No longer harmonious tones, but harsh noise
Setting out a plan of action is easier said than done
There's so many thoughts racing through my mind
The events are out of sequence
The script needs editing
My characters become aliens
Because confusion has written the lines
Interruptions weakening my skills
Concentration the only remedy

My head is pounding from the jumbled impressions
embedded in my mind
It sucks having writer's block
Take a deep breath
Tune the nuisances out once more
Set my pen to paper
Concentrate on the original idea at hand

Why Do I Keep Coming Back?

What is it that draws me nearer to you?
I think the reason may be confusing.
The pull and want has always been overwhelming.
To have what's not yours – yearning to possess
To finally know that it is yours –
fearful that possession has no real ownership
Losing what was yours – unable to let go…
Why do I keep coming back?
'Cause I never wanted to go away!
It's not as if it was easy to turn my back.
The pain growing from this agonizing distance crushes my soul.
Doubt and Anger competing with a vengeance
Sadness and Anguish winning the fight
A fight never knowing I would battle…
I keep coming back!
'Cause it puts a smile on my face to see you there on my return.
Although the hurt makes me retreat in dismay,
A compelling connection to my heart remains tethered.
Why do I keep coming back?
Confusion mingling in my mind with a conclusion…
Back is temporary and fleeting
Leaving me starving yet satisfied.

Starving for a feast I can't afford -
Satisfied for the sampling offered,
Both are a tease to my heartstrings.
So why do I keep coming back?
Understanding full well the internal conflict
The reasons why I went to start with linger on the surface.
Feelings of betrayal and not being wanted
set high in this scenario.
A crippling ache searing within each shed tear.
Only to be sedated by revisiting the unexpected welcome that awaits again and again.
Like a moth to a flame I know is my fate,
I keep coming back 'cause it's where I long to be.
Unconsciously guiding me in the direction of a heady combination of joy & pain,
Here is where I keep coming back.
Back to where the love did stray,
Back to where the love will never fade away.

Losing the Fight

My heart loss when my mind took over
I had what I always wanted but it tore my heart apart
My heart could no longer be trusted
So my mind took over the part
It told me to let go of the cause of the pain
But my heart fought for its job to remain

The End…?

If something is consistently moving forward,
Can it truly ever reach an end?
When roads are said to be closed,
There are detours that put you back to that direction.
The word 'Sorry' usually means the end of a dilemma,
But what happens if things are not forgiven?
Who's to say that it is the end?
When an exit leads you out,
You can always enter on the other side.
What makes the ending final?

Power of a Voice

With our voices heard
We will never be silenced
Word sounds have power
Rising up from the crowd
Rearing the heads of individuality
We rest in the knowledge that we have the power
Tongue lashes searing your very flesh
Leaving no visible scars
Only lasting impressions
Using our strongest muscle to tear down barriers
Heightening the muffled sounds of fear & despair
We release our strengths with courage of the mind
Rest in the knowledge that you have the power
You have the power to leave your mark
A mark that says I won't go down quiet
Telling the world "My voice will be heard"
Heard above roaring negativity
No doubt that I am a force all my own
With my voice, I have the power
With my words, I've found the strength
Within this strength, I have the power

Deserving

I have the respect of anything that crosses me
It's demanded and expected
My barking as well as my biting is what gets me noticed
Some say it's cruel and unusual
But without it I wouldn't be me, I would be you
Disrespected and ignored
My authority goes without question
My word is never challenged
My voice is always acknowledged
Positive reinforcement won't do the job alone
Fear must be instilled to make them take a second thought
A second thought about who they dare cross
After all, one man's capital punishment
Is another woman's motherly love
Never raise your voice or jab with a fist
Just a cut with the eyes to put you in your place
I love hard, but I fight even harder
Harder to gain your trust
Because respect without trust challenge my intentions
My intentions are honorable
I'm not ignored because you trust me
Trust that my respect is deserving of you

Fear vs. Trust

Fear & Trust go hand in hand.
You fear the worse and trust it will be ok.
With the ability to trust in your heart
And fear it may be broken.
How can one ever truly know love?
With fear, we dive head first into new adventures.
When in danger we trust we will be pulled to safety.
I know fear allows for caution,
However, can my trust make me blind to trouble?
Where heartache is formed by trusting what is false,
Faith is developed by overcoming your fears.
If with fear alone you never learn to trust,
Trust us the fear that will always keep you doubting.

Dazed & Confused

I'm wondering where I belong, if I fit in.
Where is my place in these surroundings?
I'm confused as to my role and dazed at the positions I fill.
Talents hidden ~ Dreams unreached
Confused & Dazed about what's blocking me,
My head is whirling from the corruption we face.
Trenching through the evils that plague our souls
Limitations enforced by superiors
Enslaved by our captures
I'm confused as to when I became a victim.
In my own home my time is not my own.
Dazing questions that puzzle the mind
Like how do you teach hate and why does love hurt?
I'm confused about the way to veer these courses.
No matter where I turn, there they'll be,
Leaving me Dazed & Confused.

I Know Where I Come From

This is where I came from
This is where I'm going
I've never forgotten my roots
They've made me what I am today
I've given myself a starting point
With a finish line that never ends
I know where I came from
I know where I'm going
Reaching for the stars
Rising to heights that are infinite
My roots are implanted deep within my soul
Able to be moved, but keeping its strong hold
They've had their beginning, but know no specific end

Inspiring Notion

Do you ever wonder what an inspiring notion is made of?
Inspiration comes from everywhere
All that we are can inspire a moment
Moments that lives with you always
Moments that travel through the breeze
Some are instant, most are infinite.
Inspiration is filled with memories
Memories that make you smile for no reason
Filled with visions of a new tomorrow
Inspiring emotions that make you sing in your heart
& shout out loud
Bringing you to create beautiful music in the key of happiness
In this world of gloom & misery
Inspiration is all around us

This Stranger I Know

I saw someone today who looked just like you
Same face…
Same smile…
Even drove the same car you drove.
I looked inside to see if it was the same person, but when I turned my head, the image was slightly altered.
This person was charming, attractive,
and understanding to my needs.
I never knew you to be this way, so it couldn't actually be you…
Could it?
I saw someone today who looked just like you.
This person was a stranger to me.
I was always taught to stay away from strangers,
but something made me want to get to know them.
Could it be the eyes?
Could it be the calming manner?
Or was it the way their hand reached out to me?
I don't know this person, but would like to find out.
Who is this stranger that seemed all too familiar?
I blinked my eyes and looked.
It was my friend ~ Someone who looked just like you.
All grown up…mature and inviting.
What was it that made me not recognize you?
How did I come to know it was really you?

Oh yeah…
It was your face…
Your smile…
The way you calmed my days and the way your hand reached out to me.
I should have known it was you!
Strange yet familiar,
I would know you anywhere.
This stranger I call my friend.

Beyond the Wall

Diversity is what separates nations
But those differences make each unique
Language & Culture
Age & Gender
Walls put up to cut off a community
But humanity grows like vines out
stretching the obstacles that lay before it
By pounding the pavement, we leave footprints for the future
All have a need to spread their wings
To soar high above with eagle eyes
Seeing further than our given sight
Tearing down the wall that divide our practices
Creating unity for a world with common goals
We unite Hearts & Minds with knowledge of self
A self that belongs to a nation that is unique
Unique because it is diverse
Diverse in its ability to Understand & Choose
Understand that we have a choice in what walls we allow to block our paths
Choose to look beyond the wall!

When You Need Your Muse

There is nothing like finding your muse.
All seems right with the world.
No job is undone. No thought incomplete. Every loss is found.
What happens when you need your muse?
Confusion and bewilderment
Procrastination on high
Feeling lost and alone
Nothing but fears and doubt to consume
Searching for the light to guide in the darkness
Traipsing through an endless labyrinth
A muse would know the combination and sequence
to open the locked entries within.
All the puzzled configurations would fit with ease.
Your muse comes when you're not looking or expecting it.
It's never when you want it.
At your lowest point, feeling the weight on your shoulders,
failure being its burden,
There seems to be no end to the vicious cycle you call despair.
When you need rescuing, it will not be
when you want a hand at difficulty.
The need will outweigh your want to be uplifted.
The want will allow you to envision the path, but your need will
bring you to the destination.
Where is your muse when you want it…?
Waiting and watching to steer you through the impossible.

Frustration

Waiting with no word and no one knows what's going on
Aggravation bringing about attitudes of disgust
Making me wait is frustrating
Being used however they please in any manner they see fit
Not being utilized to your best abilities is frustrating
Not knowing what to do or where to go
At a loss for instruction, guidance nowhere in sight
Stumbling through darkness, frustration taking over
Keep searching for a marked path leading toward the light

A Class with No Life

Rigid and Boring
Uncommunicative
Unfeeling
Low standards or High ideals
Involvement limited
Selfish and overconfident
Incompatible in workable areas
Easily distracted
Making others compromise
Where is the joy? The excitement?
Elementary teaching, belittling intelligence
Wishing for a bolt of lightning to strike
Strike into the heart of me
With my energy depleted, I need a jolt
A shock to my system
Power level low and the rejuvenating elements
are nowhere to be found
Too many foreign invaders throwing up barriers
to block my resources
Challenges are approached with much brainstorming

Beyond the Hate

I feel the anger building within my chest.
Breathing quickens, heart rate rising.
I try to move beyond the hate,
but the memory of the cause lingers.
Frustration and aggravation set in my mind,
my happy place nowhere to be found.
Living beyond the hate when there is no love to pull me through
is a struggle in itself.
There is no light to guide my way,
only darkness lies in my sight.
Pain, Loneliness, Needing…
Hatred building inside from the unsure emotions of confusion.
I'm not a hateful person and it's not in my nature to hate.
How can this fire be fueled to an unknown determination?
Whatever it is, a boiling point has been reached.
I search for an extinguisher to save me from my own danger.
Beyond the hate, pass the intense burning.

Seasoned Learner

In a world of constant improvement
There is no place to fit in the seasoned learner
Isolation from all you know
Respect for knowledge acquired is ignored
No place to call your own
Residing within, only to be seen as a visitor
Trying to collaborate, come to a compromise
Alas, assistance denied, no matter the experience

Mirror Image

With good intentions, I make sound decisions.
Working hard to insure the health of all.
Completely under the impression that life was happy
My time was free whenever needed, for who ever needed.

As I turned away from the mirror
A reflection caught the corner of my eye.
I had no clue of the image peering back with a look of confusion.
It was so eerie, because the eyes had a sadness that could not be me.

We both moved closer the glass with a puzzled expression.
With outstretched hands reaching for the other,
Our fingers touch and link with a spark.
A connection so strong the bond becomes clear.

Together made we, but I knew no knowledge of she.
"I know you. Why don't you know me?"
Her words were puzzling since surely this could not be.
I ever only glance at the mirror, no need to examine.

"I thought you to be the perfect image of me."
"You've never seen me sit and stare?"
"Never noticed me searching your eyes for a way out?"
"Do you not see my exhaustion?"
"The constant tear stained face I bare, banging my fists with a buff or shout?"

Please forgive me and do not think me rude.
If I knew we were one in the same
I would never have been so shrewd
And go as far as to neglect myself.
This happens more than I care to admit.

"How can we have this bond yet exist in two separate worlds?"
"If we are viewing our mirror image the impression should reflect the same."
"Our connection is flawless as we move in time."
"Although all that we are has no reason or rhyme."

Why have we been displaced in life...?
Made to live alternately, but together?
The reflections are mirror image to one another,
But our emotions clearly differ.

"You're always so bright and energetic."
"Breezing through the days without a tear."
"What do you do to feel so at ease?"
"A smile on your face from ear to ear."

I will admit, the days seem to be at ease
However, at times I find myself on my knees.
There is a smile I wear of course,
But somewhere in my heart, I feel it is forced.
"I think I understand your uncertainty and my overwhelming natures."
"For I have noticed your teetering hesitation when it comes to emotions."
"With every pause, I break down."

"Your struggles released, but unto me."

Why are we linked and un-tethered at once?"
What caused this sickening divide?
"I need to stop these draining situations!"
I want to feel all that I am.
How can we make each other better?
I want to know what I've been missing.
"I can't go thru this constant anguish alone."

I know emotions come at levels of risk.
They are what make one enlightened.
Without them, I am lost.
I have lived without knowing tragedy or ache,
Leaving me in ignorant bliss.

"Reflection?"
Yes, Reflection.
"Will I ever know what it feels to smile?"
I cannot answer for sure, when I'm unsure why I do smile.

Mirror Image on this wall,
Why is it that we cannot recall…?
The reason for splitting our image in two
With no restoration in sight, not even a clue
Perhaps I did not know how to handle my emotions
So they were wiped from me.
"Now I am nothing but emotion,
Never free to know the calm after each storm."

What we need is balance,

With the ability to adjust as the emotions do.
We need to merge ourselves to connect as a whole.
Linked in life, outside of the reflection.

Both turning away from the mirror
Each crying a silent prayer
"I need to know how not to feel everything!"
I need to know how to reveal what has been concealed.

Turning quickly to face the mirror
Eyes glaring intently, intentions to come were sure
With a scream so loud no sound would come
Two figures bang their fists, bound for one to become

Thrust and shutter… shards releasing tunes of emotion
Screeching, crying, laughing, sighing…
A journey of mood swings shower the images
Convulsions reflecting effects in each

An unearthly pull & squeeze attacking their frames
The fight has gone out
Now urging to let go & give in to the force was not overwhelming
A feeling of compression releases new breath
Blurred images of remembrance now clearly seen
With minds set in a spin
The whirlwind creates focus
With eyes wide, now I see…
That there are no more we!
I want to cry and now I know why.
At last, my emotions are mine and they make whole of me!

CPSIA information can be obtained at www.ICGtesting.com
Printed in the USA
BVOW08s0055161015

422748BV00001B/1/P